SHIMMERING CHAOS

(ENCHANTED CHAOS, #2)

JESSICA SORENSEN

ISBN: 9781939045348

For information: jessicasorensen.com
Cover Design by MaeIDesign

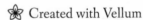 Created with Vellum

CHAPTER 1

MY ROOM IS PITCH BLACK, AND THE HOUSE *silent, except for the murmuring whispers of the wind that are begging me to come find it.*

I peel my eyelids open and climb out of bed, padding over to the window where I peer out into the night. The yard is blanketed in darkness with the trees towering in the distance.

"Can you hear me, Sky?" Vines of darkness dance around in the field just beyond the house. "Come to me. Join me. You can be my queen."

"Stop saying that," I whisper as I shiver. "I'm not your queen, and I never will be."

Darkness laughs, the tendrils hovering. "Then you'll die."

I wait for darkness to come to me, to try to take

me away, but they don't budge. They just hover in the distance, as if they can't reach me. Maybe they can't. Perhaps the spells around the house are making it so they can't get to me.

I'm safe here.

Darkness purrs with laughter. "You may be, but you have to leave eventually. Just like you'll leave the Everettsons eventually. And when you do, you'll be mine."

The tendrils shift, slipping away and giving me a better view of the trees and the road and the figures lurking in the shadows.

Hunters.

I don't know how I know. I just do.

"Now that we've found you, I'm not about to let you go," darkness warns. "You'll be mine—"

Sunlight filters in through the windows, pulling me from my nightmare. Well, and the feeling that someone is standing beside my bed.

"Hey, hey, hey, you want to know a secret?"

As my eyelids flutter open, I'm greeted by a green-eyed, hairy-faced, warty-nosed ... Well, I'm not even sure what it is.

I gasp, bolting upright and scooting across the bed as far away from the creature as I can get.

Its grey lips part, revealing a set of sharp fangs.

"Don't be afraid, little one." But the purr in its voice only spikes my fear.

Panicking, I clumsily dive off the bed, landing face-first on the hardwood floor.

"Ow," I grimace as pain radiates from my forehead.

I promptly chuck the pain aside as the thudding of footsteps hammering against the floor fills the room.

"Easy, easy, easy. I'm not going to hurt you." The creature appears near the foot of the bed, giving me a good view of its stubby, hairy legs, its short arms, and its rounded body covered by clothes that look two sizes too small for it.

"W-what are you?" I sputter as I stumble to my feet and step away from it.

It counters with a pleased grin. "An elemental protector who doesn't know what I am? Oh, what a delight!" It claps its hands in excitement and, for a faltering moment, my fear morphs into puzzlement. But then its expression darkens, its fangs growing as its eyes light up with what I can only describe as hunger. "Lucky me." Its voice is different this time, lower and rumbling with desire. Then, with a grin, it barrels toward me.

I stumble backward, bumping into the wall.

Then I let out a string of curses, jump onto the bed, and leap to the other side.

The crazy creature mimics my move, scrambling after me as I sprint for the door.

As I reach the hallway, I scan all the shut doors. With all the chaos that's been going on for the last couple of days, I never got a tour, so I'm not sure what door leads to where, except for the one the faery's hidden behind, the bathroom, and the attic. Since the Everettsons aren't your ordinary family and have things like faeries hidden behind doors, I'm a bit reluctant to just run into a random room, so I haul ass for the bathroom, figuring it's my safest bet.

My skin is scalding hot, and I can almost smell a potential fire brewing as I reach the closed bathroom door.

Crap, I need to get myself under control.

But that's a bit difficult when some odd, hairy, hungry creature is chasing me. So, by the time I wrap my hand around the doorknob, the metal melts against my skin and drips down to the floor.

Cursing my ability, I trip into the bathroom and slam the door closed. Without a doorknob, though, the door won't lock, so I press my back against it and brace myself for when the creature slams against it. Instead, an eerie stillness settles across the air that does nothing for my nerves.

Short gasps flee past my lips as I strain to listen, trying to pick up any signs of what the creature is doing. All I can hear, though, is the sound of running water ...

Wait ...

I peer around the spacious bathroom, suddenly hyperaware of the steam in the air, the foggy mirrors, and the spray of the shower running.

Oh, my God, someone is in the shower!

When Emaline showed me the bathroom, she said it was mine and that no one else would use it, so why is someone in here? Not that I'd care any other time, but right now, I care a freakin' ton!

The only positive thing about this situation is that the shower is located in the far back corner and tucked into the wall, out of view. If I could see the shower, I'd probably erupt in flames, considering it has a glass door.

As the water is turned off, my embarrassment rises to my cheeks. I rack my brain for a solution to fix this soon-to-be very embarrassing moment, but the only options I can think of are to 1). bolt out of the bathroom and cross my fingers that the creature isn't waiting out in the hallway to eat me, or 2).

warn the person who's about to step out of the shower that I'm in here. Neither choices seem fantastic, but when it all comes down to it, I think I'll take embarrassment over being eaten by some hairy, little, nubby monster.

I clear my throat. "Um ... whoever's in the shower, you might want to wait to get out."

A mortifying gap of silence passes.

"Sky?"

I cringe, recognizing Foster's voice.

It just had to be him, didn't it? Then again, I guess it could be worse. Easton or Hunter could have been in there ...

"Yeah, it's me," I reply stupidly.

"Okay." Another slamming heartbeat of silence goes by. "So, quick question. Why are you in the bathroom with me while I'm showering? Not that I mind. I'm just curious." His puzzlement is evident but mixed with amusement.

Awesome. Why do I have the feeling this moment is going to come back to bite me in the ass?

I silently beg my voice to come out evenly. "I'm not being a perv or anything," I explain defensively.

"Glad to know." Now he just sounds amused.

I release an exasperated sigh. "Some hairy,

little creature woke me up this morning and chased me out of my room. I was a little hesitant to just run into a random bedroom, since you guys hide faeries and stuff in your house, so I ran in here because I knew what was in here." I chew on my thumbnail. "Your mom said this was my bathroom and no one else would use it, so I thought it was safe to just run in."

"Oh yeah, sorry about that. Normally, no one does use this bathroom, but Porter froze the pipes in the one I normally use, so I snuck in here ... I thought you were asleep, so it wouldn't matter." He pauses. "I also thought I locked the door."

"You might've, but I melted the doorknob, so ..." I shrug, even though he can't see me.

Another pause, and then he busts up laughing.

"What's so funny?" I ask, totally lost.

"It's nothing." He works to get his laughter under control. "It's just cute ... You're cute."

Warmth consumes my cheeks. Luckily, he's in the shower so he can't see my reaction. "No, I'm not," I mutter, moving to step away from the door. "I'll step out so you can get dressed."

"No, don't," he says quickly. "Ollie's probably waiting for you to come out."

"Ollie?"

"Max's ogre ... He keeps the thing in the trunk we mentioned a few times."

"You keep an *ogre* locked in the trunk in the attic? Holy crap. Was it in the trunk when I was up there?"

"He was ... Sky, I really am sorry for the shit Easton and I did to you when you first came here. We thought we needed to get you to leave so our family's secrets wouldn't be jeopardized, but it was wrong of us."

"No, it wasn't. Or, well, wanting to protect your family's secrets wasn't. But you probably shouldn't have let me go into the attic with the ogre." I cringe as I recall how hungry he looked and those fangs ... "I'm pretty sure he wants to eat me."

"Let me get dressed, and then I'll go get Max and have him take care of him." He doesn't bother correcting me about the ogre wanting to eat me, so I'm assuming I'm correct. "Max is the only one who can really control him. Although, I'm not even sure why he's running around the house to begin with. Max usually only lets him out when he's portal traveling."

"Why? Or, well, what's the point of having an ogre?"

"Because they're good at tracking scents."

"Is there a specific reason Max needs something to track scents?"

"Because he's a tracker, which is basically like a bounty hunter in the human world."

"So, Max tracks outlaws for a living?" I mull the idea over. "What kind of outlaws? I'm assuming inhuman ones."

"Yeah, they're definitely not human," he says. "The things he tracks are usually dangerous and evil."

"Oh." Goosebumps sprout across my arms.

Quietness stirs across the air until Foster says, "So, um, I need to get out of the shower at some point."

"Oh, yeah." I mentally roll my eyes, the heat in my cheeks magnifying. "Do you want me to, um ... step out?"

"No. Like I said, Ollie might be waiting for you ..." He clears his throat. "You can just close your eyes."

I smash my lips together and restlessly thrum my fingers against the sides of my legs. He wants to get out of the shower while I'm in here? Be naked in the same room as me? Not that I think nakedness is bad; it's just a naked guy is a bit out of my comfort zone. Not that I'm going to tell Foster that.

"Just let me know when it's okay to get out," he adds with a hint of nervousness.

Never in a million years would I have thought the guy who treated me horribly the other day in the auto body shop parking lot could be so tentative and unsure. It makes the situation a bit easier to deal with.

Sucking in a breath, I close my eyes. "All right, my eyes are shut."

I hear the *click* of the shower door being opened then the rustling of clothes. Knowing that he's right there, totally naked, makes my heart rate speed up and my palms fizzle with heat.

Just calm the hell down, Sky. He's just a guy. A guy you pretty much despised until last night.

The problem is, he basically went from being an extremely cocky jerk to this nice, sweet, understanding guy who made sure I fell asleep safely in my bed. The change in him happened so swiftly that it gave my emotions whiplash. But the only reason he may be being nice to me is because I'm an elemental enchanter like him, so that kind of sucks ass. That doesn't make him any less hot, though, and knowing he's right there, without any clothes on, dripping wet, has me conjuring up all sorts of mental pictures in my mind—

"Okay, you can open your eyes now," he says with a drop of laughter in his tone.

"What's so funny?" I question, opening my eyes.

He's standing closer than I expected, his black pants hanging low on his hips and water dripping from his hair and onto his chest. His very bare, lean, tattooed chest.

"It's nothing." He sinks his teeth into his bottom lip, struggling not to smile. "But I think I may need to give you a couple of practice sessions on how to block your emotions from traveling down the link."

Wait ...

Oh shit. Could he feel the lust flowing off me when I was picturing him naked in the shower?

Do not blush, Sky. Don't you fucking dare.

I rack my mind for another topic.

"Why don't you have a shirt on?" Seriously, of all the topics I could've went with, that's the one I chose?

I need to give myself a good ass kicking. For reals.

He drags his hand across his mouth, trying to hide his amused smile. "Sorry. I wasn't expecting you to come in here, so I just brought pants to change into. I can dig the shirt I was wearing out of the hamper, though, if I'm making you uncomfortable."

"No, you're fine." I cringe at my stupid choice of words. "I mean, you don't need to put a shirt on."

He rolls his tongue in his mouth then steps toward me. My back stiffens, and he halts, his brows puckering.

"I'm not going to hurt you," he says cautiously. "I was just going to peek into the hallway and see where Ollie is."

"I didn't think you were going to hurt me ... I'm just ..." I wet my lips with my tongue and move away from the door, shaking my head at myself. So, I can handle portal traveling and dealing with my powers, but if you put me in a room with a shirtless guy, I can barely think straight. Jesus, I'm such a spaz sometimes. "I'm sorry I'm acting weird."

"You're fine." He offers me a smile then swings around me and cracks the door open.

He's within arm's reach, close enough that I can feel his body heat emitting from him, and suddenly lightning sparks across my skin. He doesn't appear to notice—thank God—as he sticks his head out into the hallway and peers around.

I inhale, and then let it out, trying to steady the overwhelming heat sweltering inside me from the sparks. But, as if his energy draws mine, my fingers magnetize toward him, and I graze his side with my fingertips, right across a tattoo of a lightning bolt. The instant my skin comes into contact with his, Foster's muscles ravel into tight knots, and a nice, big, icy-cold bucket of metaphoric water douses over me.

What did I just do?

I start to jerk back.

"No, don't," Foster whispers hoarsely, ducking back inside and reaching for my hand. His breathing comes out ragged as his gaze collides with mine, bright and lightning-blue, like the current of electricity purring across my skin.

"I just ..." I shrug. "I don't know ... Maybe ... I ..."

Despite the fact that I'm rambling and making zero sense, he seems to understand. Or, at least he nods, so yeah, there's that ...

With his gaze trained on me, he slowly draws my hand back to him and lines my palm against his side. A shaky breath falters from his lips as I splay my fingers across the lightning tattoo branding his ribs.

Lightning crackles off me and flows across him. The mixture of that and the skin-to-skin contact sends wonderful sensations throughout my body and makes me realize something. That minus a few hugs from Nina and Gage, I haven't had much physical contact. Even my parents rarely hugged me, and that revelation leaves me wondering why.

"It doesn't hurt, does it?" I ask as Foster squeezes his eyes shut.

"No, it feels ... amazing." His eyelids lift open, little bolts of electric-blue lightning reflecting in his eyes. "Do you want to feel how I feel?"

I should shake my head. I barely know him, and what I do know makes me question if we're only in here, touching each other, because I'm the only girl who can touch him this way. Plus, for me, well, I think I'm simply curious, and I know I'm attracted to him. So, I nod.

He slips his tongue out to wet his lips then carefully reaches toward my face instead of my side, which surprises and kind of disappoints me, but I'm blaming the latter on temporary loss of sanity due to extremely high body heat. Because, yeah, that's a thing ...

My thoughts become distracted as he cups my

cheek and delicate sparks kiss my skin, buzzing downward along my jawline and neck.

"Wow," I whisper as tingles break out across my flesh.

The sensation only amplifies when he moves his hand downward, along my jawline, my neck, and the curve of my shoulder. His gaze stays welded to mine as he then moves his fingers toward my side.

"You can tell me to stop if you want me to," he says as he nears the hem of my shirt.

A protest burns at the tip of my tongue, yet my lips remain fused. Again, I can't explain why. Maybe it's because our powers are connected. Or maybe it's because I'm curious about what it feels like to be touched like this.

As my lips remain zipped, he slips his fingers under my shirt and drifts upward along my side. The electricity glows brighter, humming, making my body hum with it.

"I can't ..." Foster squeezes his eyes shut, while little gasps of air rush past my lips. He lowers his forehead to mine, turning his body toward me and forcing me to lean back against the door. His chest is aligned with mine, his fingers delving into my skin as he clutches me.

I grasp on to him just as tightly as my legs wobble, threatening to give out.

Never, ever did I ever think touching someone could make me feel this ... alive.

"You okay?" Foster whispers, his breath dusting across my cheeks.

I give an uneven nod. "Are you?"

"Yeah ..." He sucks in a breath, skimming his thumb along my side. "Your skin's so soft."

I shudder. A shudder that confuses me, and the ground quivers beneath me—

"What in the hell!" someone shouts. "Which one of you is doing that?"

Foster slants back, a crease between his brows.

I blink, the daze slowly evaporating from my mind, and shift my attention away from Foster to our surroundings ...

"Holy mother of ... What the hell is happening?" I breathe out as my gaze skims along the frost webbing across the mirrors, the flames flickering in place of where light bulbs used to be, the lightning and clouds covering the ceiling, the rain sprinkling down from those clouds to the icy floor, and the tree—yes, an actual tree—sprouting from the shower, the branches swaying in a light wind.

Foster glances over his shoulder, and then his

jaw nearly smacks the floor. "Gods, this is crazy. I mean, my powers have done some strange stuff before, but this is just ..."

"Chaos?" I offer, still shocked.

Our powers did this.

We did this.

Simply because we are touching.

Jesus, what the heck would happen if we ...?

If you what, Sky? Just what do you expect to happen between the two of you?

I roll my eyes at myself.

"No, it's not chaos." He returns his gaze to mine, a smile touching his lips. "This is the most peaceful thing I've ever seen my powers create."

I cock a brow. "Peaceful? There's a tree where the shower used to be, and the ceiling is raining, and there're flames instead of light bulbs."

"I know that." He withdraws his hand from my side, causing a chill to glaze over my body. But then the heat immediately returns when he places his hands on my shoulders, moves me away from the door, and then positions himself behind me, pressing his chest against my back and molding his hands around my waist.

"That's not chaos. The rain, the frost, the fire, the tree ... Everything's in harmony with each other." His lips brush against my ear as he whispers. "It's like we created our own little elemental world, and it's beautiful."

My shoulder shudders upward as his breath caresses the sensitive spot behind my ear, and then the scene in front of me bursts with light, snowflakes blooming from the swirling clouds, the tree branches stretching, the flames dancing higher and reflecting against the ice.

"You're right. It is kind of beautiful," I admit. "It's weird, though ... seeing something so ... serene come from my powers. I've only ever created destruction before."

He grows quiet for a moment before finally saying with heavy caution, "I want to try something, okay? I don't want you to panic ... I just want to see what will happen."

I don't have a clue what he's about to do. I could—and maybe should—ask, but again, I find curiosity triumphing over my worry.

His chest crashes against my back as his breathing quickens. The snowfall thickens, veiling the room around us. Then the wind begins to whisper, breathing in rhythm with his breaths. But that's mild in comparison to when he grazes his lips along the side of my neck, a soft kiss that causes warmth to erupt in my veins.

As a gasp fumbles from my lips and my head tips back, the ice glazing the floor springs to life, crackling upward and kissing the ceiling, forming icy beams all over the bathroom.

"Gods, I think"—he struggles to breathe evenly—"with this sort of power, we could probably build a whole damn kingdom."

The fact that he may very well be right sends my pulse spiking, and the ice, wind, and the storm more than notice. They react wildly, cracking, howling, and funneling clouds of ice through the air.

"Calm down." He gently massages my hips with his fingertips. "It's okay."

"I'm trying," I say, the wind stinging my cheeks. "But it's a lot to take in. I mean, you're saying things like we could build a kingdom, and I ..."

I think I need a moment to collect myself ...

Deciding to listen to my thoughts for once, I step forward. The second Foster's hands fall from my hips, the wind stills.

As I peer over my shoulder at him, he parts his lips, but the words die on his tongue as his gaze collides with mine. Who knows what he sees? Fear and worry? If my expression matches what I'm feeling right now, then probably.

This is all so overwhelming. Only a few days ago, I thought I was the only one with powers. Now I'm standing in a bathroom with a guy who I thought hated my guts—and possibly still does—in the middle of a wintery scene that I—*we* created. I mean, how is this real life?

"I'm sorry," Foster says, paling.

I open my mouth to tell him he doesn't need to apologize, that he has nothing to do with what is sending me into panic mode, but then the door is swung open and Ollie comes rushing in.

A grin twists at his lips as he spots me.

"Ogre!" I squeak, skittering backward and pointing at the hungry-eyed creature.

The wind picks up, sending snow and ice fragments cutting through the air, and the icy floor splinters apart.

Foster whirls around, spanning his arms out to his sides as he steps in front of me, blocking me from Ollie's view.

"Move," Ollie demands through a blissful moan. "I want her. I want her now!"

"Back off, Ollie," Foster warns. "You can't have her."

"Yes, I can," he whines. "She doesn't know what I am and isn't part of Master Max's family; therefore, I can do whatever I want with her, so give her to me."

"No." Coldness chills Foster's tone as he leans back, pressing his back against me.

His scent engulfs me—warm rain, crisp snow, summer breezes, and campfire, all mixed into one scent.

A growl reverberates from Ollie. "Move out of my way, elemental protector, and give me the girl."

"If you so much as come near her, I'll break your arms and legs," Foster tells him in a low tone.

"My, my, does the youngest Everettson have their very first crush?" Ollie sneers. "How pathetic."

I peer around Foster and find Ollie grinning, and his grin only doubles when he spots me.

"You're mine," he threatens, his fangs glinting in the light.

"Fuck off," I retort, but probably only because I'm standing safely behind Foster. If it was just Ollie and me in the room, that might be an entirely different story. "I'm not yours. I'm nobody's, so back off."

Ollie's eyes flash with hunger. "Feisty. I like it. I bet you're tasty, too."

My fingers fold into fists, a comeback biting at the tip of my tongue, but Foster beats me to the punch.

"Shut up," Foster growls. "And get the hell out of here, Ollie, or I swear to the gods, you'll be punished in the worst of ways."

Ollie simply grins. "You must like her a lot. Usually, you're so neutral about everything." He pauses. "That'll make it even more fun when I rip her apart."

As an angry burst of wind circles around the room, I'm reminded of my powers. That I'm not completely weak. But everyone has been stressing how I need to keep my powers a secret. Still, though I'm a bit hesitant to allow them to slip through, I really want to, which might be a first.

"Ollie, you will *not* harm Sky," Max's commanding voice flows across the room. "If you do, you'll be sent back to your world."

Ollie must really not like his world because, in quite a panic, he sputters, "I'm sorry. Please forgive me, Master Max. I'm just so hungry and confused. I didn't realize the girl matters to you."

"Well, she does. Just as much as my brothers matter to me," Max replies, and the stupidest drop of warmth sparks inside my chest. "Remember that."

"I will, I will, I will," Ollie murmurs, his voice quieting until it fades completely as he leaves the bathroom.

"Is she okay?" Max asks, his tone crammed with concern.

"I'm not sure. He woke her up, chased her in here, and then tried to ..." Foster shakes his head, the muscles in his jaw pulsating. "What the hell, Max? Why is he out?"

"My bet is he broke the lock on the trunk again," Max says remorsefully. "Usually, it's not a big deal ... Ollie swore an oath not to harm our family when I took him in, but Sky wasn't part of that oath. It's why I was so freaked out when I found out she had been in the attic, something you and Easton did."

"I know. You don't need to remind me." Foster exhales deafeningly. "Can you make Ollie take an oath not to harm her? It'd be much better if you can."

"That's a good idea. Let me put the request in with my boss." Max gives a short pause. "Sky, you doing okay back there?"

I collect my breath before speaking. "Yeah, I'm good." Kind of feels like a lie, though. Honestly, I feel shaky and off balance. But an ogre did just try to eat me, so ...

"I really am sorry," Max apologizes again. "I'm surprised none of us felt your fear. I mean, I know we were all asleep, but still ..."

"That might've been my fault," Foster says with a bit of reluctance.

"And why's that?" Max asks, sounding positively amused. "No, let me guess. It probably has something to do with why the bathroom looks like all the worlds meshed together."

For some dumbass reason, I blush.

Is there, like, a cure for uncontrollable embarrassment? Because I could really use it around these guys.

"That's none of your business," Foster states. "Now go take care of your ogre."

Chuckling, Max leaves the bathroom.

Foster lets out a frustrated sigh before rotating around to face me. "Are you okay?"

I nod, suddenly realizing I'm clutching his

sides. I hastily withdraw my hands. Then horror sweeps through me.

"Oh, my God, I'm so sorry." I smooth the pad of my fingers along the pink, crescent-shaped marks my fingernails left on his skin. "I didn't realize I was digging my fingernails into you."

"I'm fine." The corners of his lips quirk up. "I thought we already established that earlier."

I roll my eyes. "That was lame."

"It was," he agrees with a smile. "But it got you to blush, so ..." He shrugs, his grin as bright as the flames dancing around us.

Shit, am I blushing again?

I move to cover my cheeks, but he stops me, capturing my hands in his. "Don't. It's cute."

"Stop calling me cute," I gripe. "It's driving me crazy."

His grin is all sorts of amused. "Why? It's the truth."

Good God, I can't take this anymore. Compliments are too foreign to me. All of this is.

"I need to get dressed for school," I change the subject, wiggling my hands from his grip. Then I swing around him but pause in the doorway and peer over my shoulder at him. "Is there a dress code at this school? It's an academy, right? Doesn't that mean there're uniforms?"

"Nah, we can dress however we want. But we do need to put eye drops in your eyes before we go." His muscles flex as he crosses his arms and leans his hip against the edge of the counter. "Have you decided what element you're going to go with? You need to decide really soon."

I shake my head. "Honestly, between the whole merging thing, the dreams of darkness, and waking up to Ollie hovering over my bed, I kind of forgot I was supposed to pick one."

"You can pick whatever one you want, but it might be better if you went with water, like me." He shifts his weight and massages the back of his neck. "My parents have been talking about speaking with the headmistress and requesting you be placed in as many of my classes as possible so I can guide you through how our school works and help you keep your powers hidden. Although, the school doesn't know about the last part. All they're going to know is that you're an elemental protector of whatever element you choose and that you just barely discovered your powers."

I tuck a strand of hair behind my ear. "I'm kind of glad they're doing that. This"—my gaze strays around the bathroom then back to him—"all these powers and a new, magical school ... it's a lot to take in, so I'm glad I'll have someone guiding me through it. I just hope I don't do something stupid that embarrasses you guys."

He tilts his head to the side. "How would you do that?"

I lift a shoulder. "By, like ... talking or something."

His brows pinch together. "Talking? How would that embarrass us?"

"Because I totally suck at it. So, don't be surprised if you introduce me to someone and I say something spazzy, like the first time I spoke to you ..." *Face palm.* Why did I have to bring that up? *Again.*

"It's fine. I always come off as an asshole, so maybe between your spazzy-ness and my asshole-ness, we'll ..." He wavers, contemplating.

"Make everyone avoid us?" I propose with a shrug.

He chuckles. "Maybe. It wouldn't be too bad if they did. I'm not much of a people person anyway." He crosses the bathroom toward me. "We really do need to get ready. School starts in just over an hour, but we should get there early to check you in." He moves to squeeze past me in the doorway but pauses, a nervous edge carving into his features. "And for the record, I never thought you were spazzy the first time we spoke. Not even close." Then he dips his head and my breath gets trapped in my chest.

Oh my God, is he going to kiss me? Do I want him to kiss me?

I don't know...

I don't move, don't breathe, as his lips near mine.

Right at the last second, though, he moves his head to the side and brushes his lips across my cheek.

Sighing quietly, he pushes back and leaves the bathroom without giving me a chance to say anything else.

My breath falters from my lips as I stare at him in shock, lightning bursting above me and ice melting around my feet, probably from the warmth his kiss sent through me.

CHAPTER 2

Even though Foster said the dress code was chill, I struggle over what to wear. Finally, after deciding on a pair of black jeans, a red top, and my favorite pair of red velvet boots, I head out of my room to take a shower.

When I step into the hallway, Emaline and Gabe are hovering near the bathroom.

"I'm so sorry," I apologize as I approach them. "I can try to help fix ..." My jaw nearly drops to my knees when I reach the doorway and get a good view of the bathroom.

The floor is now ice-free, the light bulbs are back, the clouds are gone from the ceiling, and a tree is no longer sprouting from the shower.

"How did everything get fixed so quickly?" I glance at Gabe then at Emaline.

Emaline smiles warmly at me. "We can control and are connected to elements, Sky. Their energy is in our blood, which means that, not only can we summon them, we can also dismiss them."

"So, you guys made all the snow and the tree go away?" I wonder why I sound so sad. It's not like I was happy Foster's and my powers destroyed the bathroom, but it was the first time my powers did something that I didn't totally hate.

"With the help of Holden, Max, and Foster, we did," she says, turning to face me. "Since you guys unleashed all the elements except for darkness, we needed one of each to be present."

"Oh. I guess that makes sense." I pause as memories of my dreams surface. "What would've happened if we had summoned darkness?"

Her smile falters. "Foster mentioned you were having dreams of it."

I nod, worry creeping through me as I remember all the things darkness said to me in my dreams. "Foster said it's normal, though."

"It is," she says, but the way she worries her lip between her teeth has me concerned. "But, since you're so new to this world and your powers, we think it might be a good idea if Foster gave you a lesson or two on how to block darkness out, okay?"

I nod. "Okay, I can do that."

"Good." She visibly relaxes then steps aside. "Go ahead and take a shower. I'll have Charlotte get breakfast started."

A protest about breakfast works its way up my throat, but knowing I'm running low on time, I smother it down and hurry inside the bathroom.

"And Sky," Emaline says as I start to shut the door. "The world that you and Foster grew? It was beautiful. If I could, I would've left it here."

Unsure of what to say, I force a smile and shut the door, pretending like I don't agree with her. But as I turn and glance around the bathroom, it looks kind of dull now.

A HALF AN HOUR LATER, I'M SHOWERED, dressed in clean clothes, and my long, brown hair has been brushed and swept to the side in a tangled mess of waves and braids. I'm not really a makeup girl, so I just dab on a bit of kohl eyeliner, some lip gloss, and call it good.

Before I endeavor downstairs, I grab my bag

and phone from my room, noting I have six missed messages.

Gage: Just wanted to check on you and make sure you're okay. You bailed so quickly last night.

Nina: Hey! Gage said you left???

Gage: You there?

Gage: I hope you didn't get in too much trouble. Let me know if you need anything.

Nina: Dude, why aren't you answering my messages?

Nina: Man, you missed it. Grey had to be taken to the hospital.

The last text makes my heart sprint in my chest as I frantically text her back.

Me: What do you mean he went to the hospital? What happened?

She doesn't answer right away, probably because it's so early. Truthfully, I don't expect her to answer until at least noon, so when I receive a message from her as I'm heading downstairs, I'm shocked. But what's in her text shocks me even more.

Nina: Dude, don't ever message me

this early again! The only reason I'm responding is because I had to get up to pee. But anyway, I'm not sure exactly what happened. From what people were saying, someone tasered Grey last night and he passed out.

Me: Is he okay?

Nina: One of his friends said he was released from the hospital, like, an hour after he was taken there, so I'm assuming he is. Seriously, though, I want to find out who tasered him and shake their hand. That asshole totally deserved it.

She's right, but that doesn't mean I feel any better about the reality. The reality that I'm fairly sure my kiss is what tasered him.

CHAPTER 3

I'M FEELING A BIT GLOOMY OVER THE MESSAGE I received from Nina. Not that I care that Grey got a little hurt. But it's hard dealing with the fact that a simple kiss from me is what did it to him.

As I exit my bedroom, with a Charlie Brown sized frown on my face, I bump into Max. And by bump, I mean literally walk right into him with so much force that I knock my head against his chin.

"Oh gods, are you okay?" Max asks as he steadies me by the shoulder.

I nod, pressing the heel of my hand against my forehead as I tip my head back and meet his gaze. "I'm sorry. I wasn't paying attention."

He offers me a lopsided smile. "Neither was I, or I would've put a stop to it before it happened."

I start to return his smile when his words click. "Wait. How would you have stopped it?"

His lips kick up into an amused grin. "With my powers."

"What sort of powers?" A memory dances in my mind of seeing glowing, green eyes my first night here. Seconds later, I fell asleep. Or, well, more like passed out. "Wait ... Did you, like, hypnotize me my first night here?"

Max pulls a wary face. "It's not really hypnotizing so much as pushing a thought into someone's mind."

"That sounds an awful lot like hypnotizing," I say with amused suspicion.

He chuckles. "Maybe you're right, and I'm sorry I did it. I just panicked when you looked out the window and saw us wandering off toward the forest."

"Where were you going anyway? To one of your"—I make air quotes—" 'tournaments?' "

He shakes his head, stuffing his hands into the pockets of his black jeans. "I was actually working that night."

"You mean, tracking an outlaw?"

His brows dart up in surprise. "How'd you know about that?"

I shrug. "Foster explained it to me after Ollie chased me into the bathroom. He said Ollie helps you track creatures."

He surveys me with a strange look on his face. "You don't sound very frightened about that fact."

"Should I be?"

"I don't know ... The creatures I track can be dangerous. And sometimes that danger occasionally follows me home." He shifts his weight, strands of hair falling into his green eyes as he tips his head forward. "Not that I'd ever let anything happen to my family, but there has been once or twice that ..." He pauses to take a breath then lifts his gaze back to me. "But yeah, anyway, that's what I do for a living and what I was doing that night when I pushed a thought to go to sleep inside your mind, which again, I'm sorry about."

"No worries," I say, even though I'm kind of wigged out. "But, who else was with you that night? I thought I saw two other figures."

"One was Ollie and the other was Porter."

"Does Porter track outlaws, too?"

Max shakes his head, his expression neutral, guarded. "No, but sometimes I ask him to help me when I'm searching for a specific creature."

His hesitancy makes me not want to ask, yet I

find myself doing it anyway, too curious to keep my trap shut.

"What sort of specific creature?"

His lips tug up into a plastic smile. "You, beautiful, curious creature, need to get going before you're late for your first day. Plus, Charlotte is making waffles, and if you don't get down there soon, you're going to miss out. And trust me; you don't want to do that." His smile turns real. "Charlotte makes the best waffles in all the worlds."

I smile back, but the move feels a bit rigid due to his purposeful avoidance from answering my question.

When I first met Porter, I sensed something was different about him, an allure flowing off him that made me dizzy. And, when we did the merging enchantment, I felt a lot of weird feelings flowing off him. In particular, there was this intense hunger to devour something. I didn't feel enough to know what that something was, but between that, the conversation with Max, I'm wondering if perhaps there's something different about the Everettson brother with the lavender eyes. The question is: what?

And why does everyone seem so hesitant to tell me?

CHAPTER 4

MAX WALKS WITH ME DOWNSTAIRS IN uncomfortable silence. I've never been good at striking up a random conversation, especially when it's pretty clear he doesn't want to talk to me. So, I let the silence be until we enter the kitchen, where a sixty-something-year-old woman with grey hair and glasses is busy cooking away. Her smile is bright and welcoming, along with the scent of waffles flowing through the air.

"You must be Sky," she greets me. She's standing near a waffle maker on the kitchen island's counter. "It's so nice to finally meet you."

I adjust the handle of my backpack higher onto my shoulder. "You're Charlotte, right?"

Her smile brightens. "The one and only cook extraordinaire."

I smile, but inside I feel miserable after hearing the news about Grey. Sure, he's an asshole and maybe deserved what happened, but him having to go to the hospital because he kissed me only cements the fact that I can't be with anyone else except Foster.

If I ever do fall in love, I want it to be with someone I connect with, who gets me, who is my other half or whatever, not the only person—creature—I can fall in love with.

Sighing, I lower myself onto a barstool beside Foster, Easton, and Max, and Foster glances up from his plate of waffles. Unlike the last time I saw him, he has a shirt on now, along with a pair of thick boots, and his dark hair is no longer wet but styled. His eyes are also silver. While he still looks gorgeous, I kind of miss the lightning-blue eyes.

"You put eye drops in already?" I quickly bite down on my tongue, my gaze skating to Charlotte.

Crap, was I not supposed to say that in front of her?

"It's fine," Foster assures me. "Charlotte is one of the few who knows what I am."

I breathe a sigh of relief then face forward on

the barstool as Charlotte sets a plate down in front of me. "Thanks," I tell her. "I don't mind serving myself food next time, though."

"And I don't mind doing my job." She hands me a fork and a bottle of syrup. "In fact, I love my job. It's way better than working anywhere in Elemental."

My brows knit as I open the top of the syrup bottle. "Elemental? That's the world where elementals are originally from, right?"

She nods as she picks up a measuring cup from the counter. "It used to be a lovely world until it started shrinking and became overpopulated."

"Worlds can shrink?" I ask, pouring syrup onto my waffles.

She nods, shoveling a cup full of waffle batter into the waffle maker. "It can when it's dying."

I gape at Foster. "Your world is dying?"

"*Our* world is dying," he corrects, twisting on his barstool to face me. "It's been going on for a while, though, so we've all sort of gotten used to the idea. Not that it sucks any less."

"Can't you do something about it? I mean, you have powers and ..." I stuff a bite into my mouth.

"It's beyond anyone's power at this point, unless someone can create elemental gods and goddesses again," he explains, adding a glob of butter to his waffles.

"Why? What happened to the other ones?"

"They died just under a couple decades ago. And since their energy created and fueled Elemental, it's now withering as the remnants of their powers fade. And only gods and goddesses are powerful enough to fuel a world."

"What about elemental enchanters? We're powerful, right? So, why can't we do it?" And why do I feel so sad that Elemental is dying?

"We're powerful, but not powerful enough for that. At least not just the two of us." His knees press against mine as he rotates sideways in his seat. "And you feel sad about Elemental dying because your powers are linked to it."

"How did you know I was sad ...?" I shake my head. "Never mind. The creepy, merge-y thing."

"Merge-y." Easton chuckles as he stands up and stretches his arms above his head. "Our sis uses funny words."

"Don't call me sis," I warn as Foster shoots him a glare and says, "You can't call her that."

Easton arches a brow at Foster, his smile taunting. "Why not, bro?"

"Because," Foster grits out, pinning him with a withering glare.

"Yeah, you're probably right. It's not a very good name for the situation." A funny look passes across his face that leaves me feeling mystified. "I think I'm going to stick with lightning eyes."

"Or Sky," I protest. "That's pretty cool, too. And it's super short so you probably won't forget it."

Easton arches a brow. "You act like I have a hard time remembering names. Like I'm a dummy or something."

I bat my eyelashes innocently at him. "Well, you do seem to have a hard time remembering mine, so ..." I give a half-shrug.

He narrows his eyes at me, but a playful glint twinkles in them. "You and I, *lightning eyes*, are going to have a lot of fun."

My lips twitch. "*Sky*. My name is *Sky*. S. K. Y. You know, like that big, blue thing that's always above us."

"That big, blue thing that you constantly strike *lightning* across," Easton stresses with a toothy grin. "So, if you really think about it, my name's more fitting."

I give him an unimpressed look, a snarky comeback tickling at the back of my throat, but Holden enters the room and interrupts us.

"Please tell me there're some waffles left," he says as he waltzes in, breathing in the syrupy air.

"I'm whipping up another batch as we speak," Charlotte replies to him with a smile.

He returns her smile then his gaze travels across the rest of us, ultimately landing on me. "Hey, Sky, can I talk to you for a minute?"

"Um ..." I shrug. Even though he seemed nice when I first met him, after he called me weak last night, I'm a bit apprehensive about Holden. "I guess so."

He gives me a small smile then signals for me to follow him as he walks out of the kitchen.

Confused, I start after him, glancing at Foster as I pass him.

He smiles reassuringly, but confusion dances in his eyes. His confusion makes me even more apprehensive.

What could Holden possibly want to talk to me about? Clearly no one else in this house appears to know.

Chewing on my thumbnail, I leave the kitchen and meet up with Holden in the foyer. He's leaning against the banister, waiting for me when I approach him.

"Hey." He straightens, scrubbing his hand across the top of his head, his eyes zeroing in on my fingernail chewing. Sighing, he lowers his hand to his side. "You don't need to be nervous, Sky. If anything, I should be nervous... Some of the stuff I said last night was uncalled for, particularly about you being weak."

"It's fine." I lower my hand from my mouth. "It's not like it wasn't the truth."

"Truth or not, I acted like an asshole." He stuffs his hands into his pockets. "And you're not weak. You just need to learn how to control your powers, but once you do, you're going to be very powerful."

"Thanks," I say, although I still feel a bit wary about this whole being powerful thing.

"It's a good thing to be powerful." It's as if he's reading my damn mind again.

"But dangerous." It's not a question. They already told me enough about my powers now that I know the more powerful I am, the more in danger I'll be.

"You'll be safe with us," he says instead of trying to sugarcoat the truth, which I appreciate.

I nod, giving him a smile. "I think I'm starting to believe that."

"Good. After what I said last night, I want to make sure you understand that." He tensely massages the back of his neck. "Sometimes I can get really protective of my family, but that doesn't give me an excuse to be a jerk."

"You weren't a jerk." A partial lie, but he apologized and I don't need to be a grudge holder. "And I think it's nice that you guys are protective of each other. In fact, there were a lot of times while I was growing up that I wished I had siblings so I could be part of a family who cared about me." God, I sound like a pathetic, mopey girl looking for a pity party.

"Well, you're part of ours now, so you no longer have to feel that way." He steps forward and gives me a hug.

Warmth spills through me, soft and welcoming.

This has happened a few times when I'm around him.

"What is that?" I ask. "That warm feeling you give off sometimes?"

His arms tense around me then he quickly

draws back. "It's nothing really. My powers some-times just have a mind of their own."

"So they just do things all by themselves?"

He nods. "Pretty much." He places his hand against the small of my back and pushes me toward the kitchen. "We should probably get back into the kitchen before East eats all the waffles."

I move forward and push open the kitchen door, stepping inside. Holden follows behind me and a grin breaks across his face at the sight of the plate of freshly made waffles on the countertop.

He hurries over and dives in,. "Thanks Char-lotte, You're the best."

She grins and stacks another waffle onto his plate.

"I'm trying not to take it personally that you always give Holden more food," Easton gripes to Charlotte. "But I kind of am." He juts out his lip. "Is he your favorite?"

"All of you are my favorites," she replies, then puts a waffle onto Easton's plate. "If you want more food, just say so,"

Easton grins then stuffs half a waffle into his mouth.

Guys and food. Seriously

I move back toward the counter where my plate is, my stomach grumbling with hunger.

Easton catches my gaze. "Are you hungry, lightning eyes? Or did you eat a baby gremlin while you were out in the hallway?"

"I'm hungry..." I pause as his words sink in. "Wait... do gremlins exist?"

They all bust up laughing, leaving me perplexed and flustered.

"Here's a little tip, lightning eyes." Easton grins at me as he gets up from the barstool and sets his empty plate in the sink. "Leaving food laying around in this house is as risky as dancing with a faerie. You're lucky I haven't eaten your food yet."

I move my plate closer to me. "There's no way you could've eaten all of these and the ones you've eaten already."

His grin widens as he rounds the counter and reaches to steal my plate from me. "I could finish these off in like thirty seconds"

I swat his hand away, and his eyes flicker with surprised delight.

Suddenly, the faucet turns on, spewing water all over the sink.

Holden chokes on a bite of waffle while Max

glances from the sink to Easton with a curious look on his face.

"I did that on purpose," Easton stresses to no one in particular, his cheeks a bit flushed.

"Sure you did." Max collects his plate in his hand while giving Easton a strange look, to which Easton responds with a glare.

Max reaches over the counter and slams the handle of the faucet down so water is no longer spewing out.

Their exchange is peculiar, but since Easton is blushing—yes, actually blushing—I think it might be better not to ask what's going on.

"You guys should get going," Max says. "You're going to make Sky late for her first day of school, and I really doubt the secretary is going to accept the I-was-late-because-Easton-and-Foster-were-bitching-at-each-other excuse." He smiles at me as he carries his plate to the sink. "I used that way too many times every time these guys made me late for school."

Smiling, I stuff a forkful of waffles into my mouth while Foster grimaces, and Easton scoffs, his blush still evident.

"Whatever, man." Easton snatches up a back-pack that's hanging on the back of a chair. "We learned our bitchiness from you, so ..." He smirks at Max then pushes through the door, exiting the kitchen.

Foster rubs his hand across the top of his head then looks at me. "Max is right. We should get going." He takes my plate with one hand then threads his fingers through mine with the other.

Max gives him an amused look and Foster sighs, steering me across the kitchen and out the door. As we enter the foyer, he hands me my plate then slips on his jacket and collects his car keys from the end table near the door.

"Isn't your mom coming with us?" I ask. "To check me in or something?"

"She has a couple of things to do this morning for work, but she'll meet us there." He zips up his jacket then takes my hand again.

I should pull away. It's weird holding hands with a guy I barely know. Yet, that's the thing. I feel like I do know Foster, perhaps from all the times I spent observing him from afar. Not that my covert gawking ever really let me discover much about him, other than he went to the auto body shop all the time. And I'm still not even sure why he was ever there.

Maybe I should just ask him. He's been so helpful with all the other questions I've had.

"Random question," I say as Foster opens the front door. "Why were you always at that auto body shop in Honeyton?"

His hand stiffens in mine, and the sky, which was the bluest I've seen it in a long time, abruptly becomes a grey overcast.

"I went there to pick up parts for my car," he mutters, then releases my hand and hurries down the stairs as if the house is suddenly on fire. Which, I guess, considering what we can both do ...

I peek over my shoulder, grateful no flames are visible. However, that doesn't explain why Foster abruptly started acting like ... well, the Foster I first met.

Sighing, I trail after him down the path and to the garage where his car is parked and Easton is waiting in the back seat.

Foster ducks into the driver's seat then shuts the door and starts up the engine.

Balancing the plate of waffles in one hand, I open the passenger door and lower my head to glance in the cab at him. "Let me eat this really quick first." I hold up the plate of waffles. "I don't want to get your car sticky."

"I don't care if you get my car sticky." He avoids eye contact with me, cranking up the heat. "We need to go or we're going to be late."

I glance at the plate, and then at his nice, clean leather interior. "Maybe I should just leave the waffles here."

Shaking his head, he finally looks at me. "Sky, just get in the car. With how much you're going to be using your powers today, you need to eat or you're going to be weak. And I'd rather you get my car sticky than for you to come off as weak on your first day of school."

Easton lets out a snicker. "You guys should really start paying more attention to what you're saying. All this sticky talk sounds so dirty that it's starting to make me feel sticky."

Foster rolls his eyes. "If you don't cut this whole jokester shit out, I'm going to tell Sky why you were blushing in the kitchen and why the water turned on."

Easton's smile quickly dissolves. "Shut the hell up."

"Then you," Foster quips, catching Easton's gaze. Easton glares back at him but smashes his lips together and remains silent.

Foster's gaze settles on me, his expression softening. "I promise I don't care if you eat your breakfast in here. It's just a car, Sky."

"Oh, fine." I climb in and shut the door, balancing the plate on my lap while I strap on the seatbelt. "A very pretty car, though."

A smirk curls at Easton's lips as he digs his phone out of his pocket. "A girl who's into cars? Dude, I think Foster just crea—"

"Don't finish that sentence," Foster cuts him off, throwing Easton a sharp look. "I swear to the gods, I'll tell her."

Easton pulls a mocking face. "Whatever. I'm just saying the truth. And this is payback for the many times you gave me shit about the girls I hooked up with."

Foster's lips part then shut, his shoulders slumping. "Fine. But just lay off it for a while, or else I'm going to tell her."

"I'll try." Easton hammers his fingers against his screen as he types a message.

They grow quiet after that as Foster turns back around in his seat.

"So, you're really not going to tell me what embarrassed Easton?" I ask as the secrecy starts to taunt me.

Foster shakes his head, his gaze skating to me. "Trust me; it's better if you don't know."

I crinkle my nose. "I'm not so sure I agree with you."

Foster gives me an apologetic look, then shifts the car into reverse and starts to back out of the garage. "This is sort of random, but I'm curious; have been curious about this for a while." He pauses as he turns the car around and drives down the driveway. "That day you approached me and asked about my car. Did you know what year my car was and you were just pretending not to?"

"Yeah, I knew what year it was ... My dad, he's really into classic cars." I stab the fork into the waffles. "If I hadn't known, I wouldn't have taken the time to look it up." I pop a bite of waffle into my mouth. "I wasn't that eager to impress you."

"Sure you weren't." He tosses me a teasing smile.

"I actually wasn't. My friend Nina convinced me to do it, and I only did it because she pointed out that you weren't from Honeyton, so the outcome wouldn't matter because I probably wouldn't see you again." I stuff another chunk of waffle into my mouth, mostly to distract myself from my internal embarrassment. "Go figure you ended up being the son of my new guardian. Seriously, it's like fate hates me or something."

He slows to a stop as he reaches the edge of the driveway, staring ahead at the road. "Does it hate you, though?"

I'm not even positive if he's talking to me or himself. Still, I almost reply with a *yes*, especially after he got so irritated with me for no damn reason when I asked him why he was at the auto body shop. But I can't bring myself to say so.

The truth is that me ending up with the Everettsons isn't necessarily a bad thing. I'm starting to see that now. In fact, I feel more weightless than I ever have, able to embrace my powers instead of despising them.

CHAPTER 5

THE THREE OF US REMAIN QUIET AS FOSTER drives toward the shallow hills that border the town. As we drive, Easton has me rest my head on the console so he can put eye drops into my eyes after I announce I'll go with water as my element.

"Please don't play with my eyes again," I tell Easton as he leans over me. "I hate my eyes being touched."

The edges of his lips quirk. "But they're so pretty. I just want to touch them all the time."

"That is seriously the creepiest thing I've ever heard," I say, wiggling around to get comfortable.

He presses his hand to his chest, mocking being offended. "I tell you your eyes are pretty and all you say is that my compliment is creepy. Wow, that's cruel."

"Touching eyes is creepy," I insist. "Although, I doubt you think so since you have a bunch of eyeballs in your fridge."

"Hey, I do think that's creepy," Easton gives an exaggerated shudder. "If I had my way, Hunter and Holden would keep their science supplies in another fridge, way, way far away from the house. Preferably in another world."

"Remember that one time they put a jar of demon tongues in there?" Foster says, his face contorted in disgust.

"Wait..." My eyes nearly bulge out of my head. "Demons exist?"

"Um..." Foster trades a look with Easton, who gives a shrug.

"Don't look at me." He rolls up the sleeves of his shirt. "You're the one who said it."

Foster sighs. "I know." He looks at me. "Yeah, they exist. But there's not a lot of them around, so you don't need to worry."

"Are there some in this world?" I ask worriedly, acting the opposite of what he told me to do.

"Yeah, but elemental protectors have a sixth sense that lets them know when a demon is present, so demons tend to avoid being near us," he explains, cranking up the heat.

I still don't feel any better. I mean... Demons? *Demons?* "What do they look like?"

"The ones that are here in this world take on a human form," Easton replies, unscrewing the cap off the eye drops. "But in their true form, they come in all different shapes, sizes, and colors. Some have scales. Some have slimy skin. It really depends on what kind of demon they are."

"Gross," I mumble, causing Easton to chuckle.

"Yeah, definitely gross," he agrees then wiggles the bottle of eye drops in front of my face. "All right, we're almost to the school, so it's time to get those pretty eyes of yours hidden."

Pretty eyes? Is he for reals?

As if sensing my thoughts, he grins. "Your eyes or gorgeous whether you think so or not. And trust me, I'm not the only one who thinks this," He glances at Foster then holds my eye open with his fingers. "Now hold still."

I do what he says and then he puts the drops into my eyes. Once my eyes are nice and silvery, looking really freakin' weird in my opinion, I rest back in the seat and work on finishing my breakfast while taking in my surroundings.

The road we're driving down is desolate, only a house or two here and there, with mostly trees and spacious fields.

"Is this the town?" I wonder after I've finished the last of my waffles.

"Nah. The town's that way." Easton nods toward the left. "You can't see it right now because of the trees and stuff, but even if they weren't there, it's hard to see." He rolls the sleeves of his shirt up. "It's a really small fucking town."

"That's what Max said." I squint against the sunlight streaming through the clouds. "I want to get a job, but Max said it'd be hard for an out-of-towner to get one."

"I think you should be okay now that you have powers," Easton tells me. "When Max said out-of-towners, he actually meant humans."

I rest my arms on the console. "But humans live here, right? So, how do they work?"

"Most of them work at the factory on the outskirt of town," Easton explains, combing his fingers through his hair.

"And they never wonder why they don't get hired elsewhere?" I question skeptically.

"They probably would if it wasn't for us keeping most of the other shops invisible with magic—they don't even know most of the places in town exist." Easton winks at me. "You need to stop thinking like a human. Nothing is simply black and white. In fact, this world is like a damn fucking rainbow with sparkles and everything."

"I'm starting to realize that, but I've also spent most of my life thinking I was human, so it's sort of hard to break the habit of thinking like one," I explain then pause. "What I don't get, though, is how it seems like it'd be so much easier for you guys to just live in your own world. I mean, I know Charlotte said it's overpopulated, but still, hiding your powers is a pain in the ass. That I understand."

"It's not just overpopulation that makes Elemental so unlivable," Foster says, downshifting as he prepares to make a turn off the highway and onto a paved road that weaves between the trees. "It's become corrupt because of overpopulation and the increase of elemental protectors of darkness." He flips on the blinker and turns onto the road. "It's like that for a lot of worlds, which is why we came here. Although corruption is spreading here, too, like with the hunters."

I swallow the lump wedged in my throat. "Why the increase in corruption everywhere?"

The air grows so still I can hear the beating of my own heart.

"In Elemental, it's because all the gods and goddesses died. Well, except for one," Foster says, tightening his grip on the wheel. "The god of darkness is still alive, so his power has become more prominent."

A shiver crawls over my body. "Really?"

He nods, his knuckles whitening. "He's also the god responsible for my grandparents' deaths." He shifts the car and decelerates as we reach the trees. "It's been the god of darkness's mission to eliminate all the elemental enchanters in our world because, if there were more of us, we could potentially overthrow him and rid the darkness plaguing our world, which he put there. Of course our kind can't solve the problem of our world dying since only gods and goddesses can feed energy to it."

"How did they die?" I whisper, tears pooling in my eyes for some bizarre reason. "I mean, the other gods and goddesses."

"No one knows for sure, but some have speculated that the god of darkness killed them so he could rule on his own." Foster glances at me, a frown tugging at his lips. Then he reaches across the console and brushes his fingers across my cheek. "Sky, don't cry. I promise nothing will happen to you. You're safe with us."

As he grazes my cheekbones with his knuckles, I realize tears are dripping down my cheeks.

"I'm sorry. I don't know why I'm crying." Mortified, I wipe my face with the back of my hand.

"It's perfectly fine." He brushes strands of hair out of my face. "You're handling this better than most."

"I doubt that." I rub my eyes, my heart feeling strange, as if a piece has fallen out. "I wish there was something that could help Elemental. It'd be nice to see it one day."

"It was beautiful once." He steers down the road with one hand, resting his other on my cheek. "My parents work for the elemental protector organization, and they've been working on finding a new source to feed our world ever since the gods and goddesses died. They've had a couple of findings, mostly in books and folklore told amongst our kind that suggests that, before the gods and goddesses died, they hid power sources that contained each of their own powers. But, so far, there hasn't been any proof, so it's mostly just an urban legend."

"You and I both know it's probably just stories." Easton slides forward and crosses his arms on top of the center console. "If the gods and goddesses left their power sources behind, someone would've found them by now."

"You never know. We used to believe there weren't any other elemental enchanters, so ..." He shrugs, looking ahead.

I track his gaze, and my eyes widen.

Just in front of us, the trees open up to a flat, flowery field that stretches as far as the eye can see. And smack dab in the middle of it is a towering, gothic-like building, three stories high with turrets and everything.

"Is that the academy?" I gape at the building in astonishment.

Foster nods. "Yep, that's your new school."

The corners of my lips twitch upward. "It's actually really awesome looking."

Smiling, he steers through the iron-gated entrance. "Just wait until you see the inside."

My smile enlarges until we turn into the parking lot. Then my mood nosedives.

"There're so many people here," I note, peering around at all the cars and trucks and the people wandering around. But, are they even people?

"This is the elemental protectors' section." Foster parks in the first open spot available, silences the engine, and then points to the left at a smaller building in the distance that has a domed roof and an arched entryway. "That's where the humans attend and where you'll go for your human-related classes, like math and English."

"Our building is better," I remark, unfastening my seatbelt.

The smile that consumes his face is a combination of amusement and elation.

"What's that smile for?" I slip my bag over my shoulder and reach for the door handle.

"It's nothing." He collects his car keys and shoves open the door. "You just referred to it as *our* school, like you've accepted you're part of it."

Wow, he's right. I hadn't even noticed.

Unsure of what to make of that—that I'm beginning to accept this new life of mine and so quickly—I decide not to make anything of it, just let it be, and hop out of the car.

The instant my feet touch the asphalt, the gawking starts. Everyone within a fifty-foot radius glances in my direction with curious eyes.

Awesome. This is a socially awkward person's nightmare.

Summoning a tremulous breath, I round the front of the car toward the driver's side where Foster is waiting for me.

"This is worse than I thought it'd be," Easton comments as he climbs out and joins us, slinging his bag over his shoulder then slipping his hands into his pockets and glancing around at all the gawkers. "Gods, people need to get a life. So there's someone new? It doesn't give them the right to stare like a bunch of nosey fuckers."

"Why are they staring?" I ask, sidestepping closer to Foster when a huge guy with bulky muscles and lavender eyes winks at me.

Ice. He's an elemental protector of ice.

"Fresh meat." Easton winks at me then grins when I pierce him with a look. He chuckles, but then huffs out a sigh. "It's probably partially our fault everyone's staring. We have some friends and everything, but we don't spend a lot of time with anyone outside our family's circle. And we've never brought anyone to school with us before."

"Awesome," I grumble. "I hope they stop soon. I hate being the center of attention."

Easton rolls his eyes. "Yeah, that's not going to happen, sweetheart."

"Unless maybe I'm not around you guys," I point out. Although, the idea of starting this new school without them makes me want to barf.

"They're still gonna stare at you even if you aren't." When puzzlement dances through me, Easton lightly tugs on a strand of my hair. "You're new, which draws attention. And you're pretty."

I resist an eye roll. "Nice try, flirt, but I spent my entire life being either invisible or tormented, so I know you're full of sh—"

He places a finger over my lips, shushing me. "I'm going to stop you right there. You're pretty, and I'm sure you haven't been invisible. You're just shy. I got that from the first time I met you. But I think your shyness quickly wears off once you've been around someone for a bit, especially someone who's sexy as hell and likes to push your buttons." He winks at me, his grin cocky.

I disagree with him about me being pretty. Sure, I don't think I'm ugly, but my looks are average. Not that I care. It's not like my life is going to be easier if I suddenly become this beautiful swan. My life is my life, and I am who I am, whether I'm pretty or not.

"And as for being tormented," Easton continues, lowering his finger from my lips. "My bet is it was from guys who thought you were hot but got pissed off when you wouldn't give them any attention."

My lips curve downward as his words sink in. "If that's true, then some guys suck."

"Some do," Easton agrees with a nod. "Foster and I aren't those kinds of guys, though. Just FYI."

"You were pretty douchey when I first met you," I remind him, adjusting the handle of my backpack.

He shakes his head. "Nah, I wasn't douchey. I was just trying to protect something."

"You mean you're family?"

His attention fleetingly skates to Foster then back to me. "Sure."

My brows crinkle as I glance between the two of them. Why does it feel like there's more they're not telling me?

Foster and Easton share another look, and then Foster shakes his head, the muscles in his jaw pulsating. Then his forehead creases as his phone buzzes from inside his pocket. Fishing it out, he glances at the message then stuffs his phone away and looks at me.

"My mom can't make it today," he tells me. "Her and my dad got called on a couple of different missions, and they're going to be gone for at least the day."

"What mission did they get called on?" Easton asks, glancing at his phone.

"I'm not sure." He shrugs, but another look passes between them.

My gut warns me that they're definitely keeping stuff from me. A lot of things.

"So, who's going to check me in to school?" I ask, deciding I've had enough of their secret, silent conversations for now. "Or, should I just start tomorrow?" *Please say the latter, because this is starting to become too much.*

"My mom called the school, and they agreed to let her come in when she gets back from her mission and sign all the paperwork. So, all we need to do today is stop by the main office and pick up your schedule and class supplies. And you should be in all the same classes as mine. Well, mostly the human ones since a lot of my elemental-related courses have prerequisites." He scratches the back of his neck. "But, if you run into any trouble at any time, you can either text me or send for help down our link."

"You're acting nervous right now ..." I edgily glance around the parking lot, the building, and ultimately at the people. "Is it not safe here?"

"No, it is ..." But Foster's heavy reluctance has me concerned. "The school and the walls around it have a ton of powerful protection spells, so only permitted creatures can come here. It's almost as safe as our house. I just want to make sure you send for help if someone bothers you. I—we want to make sure you're as comfortable as possible dealing with this new world and learning about your powers."

"Thanks, but ... is your house really safer than a school full of elemental protectors?" I question, because the idea seems a bit crazy.

"My brothers and I are very powerful. In fact, we're pretty badass." Foster winks at me, and my traitor stomach does kick flips. As if he knows exactly what's going on inside me, and maybe he does, he smiles then nods toward the building. "Come on; let's try not to be late."

I begrudgingly nod, and then we start to make our way across the parking lot and toward the school. With every step I take, the staring increases and my nerves skyrocket to the point where clouds are rolling in.

As we reach the wide stairway that leads to the double-doored entrance, I just about turn around and bolt as a group of people with the most striking dark eyes appear at the top of the stairway.

Elementals of darkness. I'm not even sure how I know, other than I can sense the darkness flowing off them.

In response to my nerves, lighting lights up the sky like a goddamn blue strobe light.

Foster hastily laces his fingers through mine and guides me closer to him, static buzzing between us.

"You're fine," he assures me. "Easton and I won't let anything happen to you."

Still feeling shaky inside, I latch on to his hand.

"You need to relax," Easton whispers. "Don't let them sense your fear."

I take a deep breath and another, but my pulse remains jittery.

"You've got Foster and me right here," Easton says. "No one's going to hurt you."

I only relax again after we pass by the elemental protectors of darkness, finally entering the school.

"Holy ... Wow," I breathe out as I take in the cathedral ceiling painted with the colors of the elements, the glittering chandeliers, and the black and white checkerboard floor. Everything is extravagant from the trimming on the walls to the intricately shaped doorknobs. It looks like a museum or a castle and not a school, especially since ... "Where are all the lockers?"

"We don't have any." Foster tightens his hold on my hand as he squeezes by people congesting up the hallway and heads toward a wide door labeled: *main office.* "The books we use stay in the classrooms, along with most of our supplies and stuff."

"I'll catch up with you in a bit," Easton says, coming to a stop. "I have to go talk to a teacher about making up a final." He gives me a smile before taking off in the opposite direction Foster and I are headed in.

Foster throws a wave at him, his attention fixed on getting us to the main office. He acts entirely unaware of how much everyone is staring at me— no, *us*—now. More in particular, our interlocked fingers.

I should pull away. We're not by the elemental protectors of darkness anymore, and it might make the staring dwindle if I do, but I worry what my powers will do if I break the ease he's instilling inside me , worry I'll lose control over my powers. After spending years struggling to keep my powers hidden, I like that I have a bit of help now. Not that I want to rely on him completely. One day, I want to be able to control my powers as well as he does.

"If there're no lockers, then why the heck did I bring a backpack?" I ask as he pulls open the door to the main office.

"You'll need it for your human classes and to carry around the supplies you can't leave in class," he says, tugging me into the main office.

The space is quaint and lined with bookshelves and a couple of antique desks. The walls are decorated with artwork of scenes that I'd assume belonged in fantasy novels, except now I know other worlds exist, so maybe the places are real.

Since the secretary is nowhere to be seen, we have to wait. We're not alone, though. A group of guys are sitting in chairs near the front desk, chatting with each other and laughing. All their eyes are brightly colored and match one of the elements, letting me know they're not human.

One of them smirks at Foster when he notices him; his golden eyes announcing he's an elemental protector of fire.

"Well, well, well, this is interesting." With a chillingly wicked smile on his face, he leans forward in the chair, his brown hair falling into his eyes. "Did the perfect Foster get in trouble for the very first time?" He spats the word *perfect* like it's repulsive.

Perfect Foster? The guy standing beside me, dressed in black and covered in studded accessories, is known around this school as perfect? I mean, look-wise, sure, he's gorgeous, but his personality ...? Well, it all really depends on which Foster we're talking about: the one I first met or the guy holding my hand and helping me deal with everything.

I sneak a questioning look at Foster, to which he heaves a sigh.

"Just ignore him," he tells me. "He's an asshole. And a stupid one at that."

"Fuck off," the guy growls, rising to his feet and crossing his arms. "Just because you think you're the shit doesn't mean you are." He steps toward us, his eyes darkening and his fingers sparking with bright-orange flames. "And one day, I'm going to make you realize that you're a pathetic piece of shit." Smoke hisses from his skin. "Just you wait."

Wait. Can he use his powers on us right now?

No one ever explained if we could use them at school or not.

"Go ahead. And while you're at it, go ahead and use your powers on me," Foster says calmly, but edginess currents off him and, in the distance, thunder crashes. "Like I'm afraid. Your powers are weak as hell."

"Wanna find out?" The fire guy raises his hands in front of him, the flames on his fingers erupting and causing smoke to funnel through the room.

"Brody, dude, what're you doing?" One of the guys who was sitting with him jumps to his feet and places his hand on Brody's shoulder. "You're already on probation for the last time you used your powers without permission. If you do anything else, you're going to get kicked out."

Brody's blazing gaze remains seared to Foster. "So what? This asshole deserves to get his ass fried for what he did to Sofie."

Who the heck is Sofie?

"I didn't do anything to Sofie but turn her down," Foster states in a glacial tone I've heard him use many times. Well, up until he found out what I am. "And she—and you, apparently—need to get over it."

"You led her on then broke her heart," Brody bites out, the flames spreading furiously up his arms. "She hasn't been the same since."

"I never led your sister on." Foster's fingers twitch in mine as smoke pours thickly around the room. If it keeps up, it's going to become hard to breathe. "If she told you that, she lied."

Knowing what I know about Foster, I doubt he's lying. That doesn't mean he wasn't a jerk to this Sofie when he rejected her—that's coming from my own experience. Still, that doesn't give Brody the right to set him on fire or whatever he's about to try to do to Foster.

"Sofie doesn't lie," Brody growls, stalking toward Foster. "I should fry your ass right now. Scar your body with burns like you scarred Sofie's heart ..." He pauses, the flames extinguishing when he notices mine and Foster's intertwined fingers. "And who is this lovely, little thing?" His lips curl into a twisted grin as his gaze zeroes in on me.

I fuse my lips together and shrug.

"Oh, I'm going to get an answer out of you." He grins, his golden eyes shadowing like smoke over a flame. "And I'm going to enjoy it while I do it."

As heat flares through my veins, Foster jerks his hand from mine and strides toward Brody.

"If you so much as touch her, I'll make your life a living hell." The coldness in his tone glazes the air. "And so will my brothers."

Brody's Adam's apple bobs as he swallows, but then he recovers rapidly and plasters on a grin. "Go ahead. You don't scare me, and neither do your stupid brothers." Brody gets in Foster's face, lowering his tone. "Your family may have this entire school wrapped around their fingers, but you don't have me fooled. And one day, I'm going to make you pay for breaking Sofie's heart and show you how she felt when you did it."

They stare each other down, heat and frost lingering in the air and making my brain dizzy. Who knows what would've happened if a woman with chin-length, black hair hadn't walked in?

"Gentlemen, is there a problem?" she asks, glancing at Foster and Brody.

"No ma'am," Foster tells her while Brody says, "Nope. We were just talking."

Sighing, the woman walks over to the desk and drops the stack of papers she was carrying.

When her back is to them, Brody hisses, "This

isn't over, Everettson. I'm going to make you burn and enjoy every moment of it."

"And I'll fucking drown your insides if you so much as come near Sky," Foster warns lowly.

Yep, Sky, you're definitely not in human territory anymore.

CHAPTER 6

So ... things aren't going as well as everyone seemed to believe it would.

Foster and I are sitting in front of the secretary's desk, listening to her explain why I'm not allowed to take any elemental protector classes, even the basic ones. That, because I'm a senior and just barely learned I have powers, there's no way I'll ever be able to catch up in any of the element-related classes, and I need to just take all human classes and finish up the year.

"She needs to take some elemental classes," Foster insists, restlessly tapping his foot on the floor. "She needs to learn about our world and how to control her powers."

"Foster, I understand this is frustrating, but

you need to think of the bigger picture." The secretary—Anna as she told me to call her—leans forward and overlaps her fingers on her desk. "It's the last semester before graduation and, with her limited knowledge of our world, there's no way she'll be able to pass any element-related classes."

"My mom already talked to the headmistress," he continues to argue. "And she agreed Sky could take a couple of basic elemental classes."

"I understand that, but the headmistress didn't fully understand Sky's limited knowledge of our world when she agreed to that." She turns the computer screen toward us. "I just emailed her the information you gave me on Sky, and this is what the headmistress replied with. You can, of course, request a meeting with her to discuss it further, but unfortunately, she had to leave this morning to attend an emergency meeting in Elemental."

Foster frowns at the message on the screen that basically states I won't be allowed to attend elemental classes. "Fine, we'll schedule a meeting with her. One that my mother will attend."

"Very well." Anna frowns, clearly annoyed. "Have her call in so I can set up a date. But it won't be for at least a few days until the headmistress gets back. Until then, Sky will have to attend these scheduled classes." She hands me a piece of paper with a list of basic classes—pre-calculus, English, biology, etc.—along with what looks like a standard P.E. uniform—shorts and a shirt with the school's name on it. "I put her in as many of your human classes as I could," she tells Foster. "But not all of them were available."

Foster grinds his teeth as he pushes to his feet, shooting her a dirty look before taking my hand and pulling me to my feet.

We leave the office, with my schedule and P.E. uniform in hand, and head outside toward the other building where our first class is held, which we fortunately have together.

The sky is grey, the air chilly, and a bit of frost glazes the grass. The parking lot is vacant, though, for which I'm grateful, but our tardiness means I have to walk into class late and that will probably draw attention.

"I'm sorry about this," Foster says as we make our way up the path that leads to the domed building. "Hopefully, my mom can get everything fixed."

"It really is okay. I kind of get where the headmistress is coming from. I know nothing about our world or my powers and trying to jump into any classes related to them at the end of our final year would more than likely result in me failing. Although, it would've been nice to learn more about my powers and the history of our world."

"You *will* learn about them," he assures as we reach the entrance door. "If my mom can't get the headmistress to budge, my brothers and I'll teach you everything you need to know."

"That seems like a lot of work for you guys, and all because you got stuck with me."

"We didn't get stuck with you."

I arch my brows. "Um, yeah, that's exactly what happened."

He studies me intensely. "Maybe you're right, but that doesn't mean we mind. In fact, we like having you around."

"Yeah, yeah." I roll my eyes, but on the inside, my stomach does that stupid fluttering thing again. "We'll see if you're still saying that after you've been around me for a while."

He continues to study me, appearing like he wants to say more, so I'm thrown for a turn when he abruptly changes the subject.

"I'm sorry about Brody bothering you this morning." He pulls open the door to the school.

"It's fine." I step inside, and he follows behind

me. Unlike the other building, lockers line the walls and the ceilings are peaked and lined with beams. "It's not like I never had to deal with a douchey guy before."

"Yeah, I know, but ..." He stuffs his hands into his pockets. "You're already nervous enough as it is. You didn't need my drama added to it. And the way he threatened you ..." He shakes his head with his jaw clenched. "He's not going to touch you. I won't let it happen."

"I'm not going to let it happen either," I say as confidently as I can. "I know I don't have much control over my powers, but I'm not completely helpless. I've handled crazy situations before. My parents used to bring all sorts of sketchy-ass people home with them, and the stuff they tried to do ..." Wait. Why am I telling him this? I haven't even told Nina and Gage this stuff. "But anyway, yeah, I can take care of myself."

Pity flashes in his eyes. "Well, even if you can, I don't want to be that person in your life who forces you to handle things."

I want to feel good about what he said, but I still don't know why he's being nice to me. Honestly, I'm not sure if I'll ever know.

"That's great, and I appreciate it, but I just

want to make sure you understand I'm not totally incompetent," I tell him.

"I've never thought you were incompetent, no matter what I may have said."

I wish I knew if he was being truthful. Wish I knew a lot of things.

"Good." I sink my teeth into my bottom lip as we slow to a stop. "I'm kind of curious why Brody thinks you broke this Sofie person's heart, though."

Foster's shoulders sag as he sighs. "It's a long story, but basically, she's this girl who's been trying to get me to go out with her for a couple of years. At first, she just flirted with me. But then things got really weird when she broke into my room and waited for me on my bed in nothing but her under-wear." He slips his hands from his pockets and fiddles with the clasp of a leather band on his wrist. "I'm not going to lie. I was a dick to her and prob-ably could've handled the situation better, but sometimes, it's hard ... I've been forced to be so cold and indifferent for so long that I forget what emotions feel like and that most creatures and humans do have them."

My heart aches for him. "I'm sure you have feelings, too."

"I do, but they've been buried for so long that I sometimes forget what they're like."

"I kind of get where you're coming from. Or, well, I know what it's like to have to force myself to stop feeling things because I worry the sky might erupt in flames. Honestly, I'm not sure I've ever *really* felt. I've always kind of had to rein in my emotions."

He hesitates. "Do you ever wonder what it's like? To just *feel*?"

"Sometimes," I admit. "But I'm kind of afraid, too."

His gaze flicks to my lips, his eyes burning with what I think is desire. The floor quivers and panic sets in. But when Foster takes my hand, the shaking slowly stops, along with the panic.

"Me, too ... I've thought about it a lot. What it would be like to feel what I want ... to have what I want ..." He leans in, as if to kiss me.

And part of me wants to let him. Wants to feel his lips against mine. Wants to let everything I've ever kept buried deep inside me out. But the other part of me questions if he'd even want to kiss me if I was the human girl who tried to hit on him that day in the parking lot.

My heart slams against my chest as I turn my head. "I'm sorry," I mumble.

He takes a steadying breath. "It's fine." When I refuse to make eye contact with him, he sketches a path along the inside of my wrist. "Sky, I promise it's fine. I probably shouldn't have tried to kiss you anyway. Not here and not now and not when you don't want to."

Sucking in an inhale, I meet his gaze.

He offers me a small smile. "We should get to class. We're already pretty late."

I nod, grateful he isn't making a big deal out of this, unlike my heart that seems super peeved at me right now.

"So, we have this class together, but not the next class, right?" I ask, desperate for a subject change.

"Yeah, my next class is History of the Water Element." He pulls a face.

"Is it a boring class?" I wonder.

"No, it's okay ... but sometimes it sucks not being able to attend classes that actually pertain to my element."

"So, there's none at all for ... well, what we are?"

He shakes his head. "As far as most know, our

kind is extinct ... It almost was," he adds as an afterthought, glancing at me.

It starts to hit me then just how rare we are. Rare in even a magical world. And I can't help wondering how much of my kind had to die for things to become this way.

As I enter the classroom with Foster, my thoughts shift as thirty sets of eyes glance at me. Curiosity sparkles in some of them, while others carry disdain. It makes me want to turn around and run. I'll go to Nina's and hide out, spend my days doing whatever I want, just like I used to. I wish I could do that, but knowing what I know now ... everything's changed.

I've changed.

When I went to the Everettsons', it changed everything. It changed me. It changed the life I once knew.

But maybe that life never existed to begin with.

FIRST PERIOD ISN'T TOO AWFUL, BUT MAINLY because Foster is in it with me. I'm a bit apprehensive about my second class, but when I walk in, relief washes over me as I spot Easton sitting at one of the desks. He smiles at me when I enter.

"Aw, look, it's my favorite creature in all the worlds," he teases as I drop my bag onto the desk beside his.

I lower my ass into the seat. "Do you ever let up?"

"Let up from what?" he asks innocently, but with a twinkle in his eyes.

"Hey, East." A girl with long blonde hair waves at Easton as she walks into the classroom. But her smile falters when she notices me. "Who's this?"

"This is Sky." Easton gestures at me.

The girl's forehead creases as she stops beside Easton's desk. "Is she the girl that's living with you?"

"Yeah. And FYI, you can ask her questions directly," Easton tells her with a teasing grin. "She can totally hear and even knows how to speak. It's seriously the most miraculous thing I've ever seen." He winks at me.

I roll my eyes at him for probably the tenth time today.

"Oh... yeah... right." The girl forces out a high-pitched laugh, then she sticks out her hand in my direction. "Hey, I'm Jane. It's so nice to meet you."

I shake her hand, highly aware that she grips the shit out of my fingers.

Either this girl has got super strength or she's pretending to like me.

"It's nice to meet you too," I manage to get out then pull my hand away from her's, resisting the urge to massage my aching fingers.

She gives me an exaggerated friendly smile. "We should totally hang out sometime. I know how hard it is to make new friends."

"Okay, yeah. That sounds awesome. Thanks." I force a smile and try not to squirm, but her crazed smile is really starting to creep the hell out of me.

"Awesome." She gives me one last fake smile then turns to Easton, a real smile settling on her lips. "Are we still on for the party this weekend?"

"Actually, I'm not sure if I can go. I may have to do some family stuff," Easton replies, half distracted by his phone.

Her smile fumbles, but she hurriedly plasters it back on as he glances up at her. "Well, let me know if you're down. Tammy's party is going to be amazing." She waggles her fingers at him then she takes a seat in a desk a few rows up and leans over to talk to girl with long, brown hair sitting the desk across from her.

"Is that your girlfriend?" I ask, trying to ignore the subtle nasty glances Jane and the brunette are giving me.

Easton shakes his head and stuffs his phone into his pocket. "We're just friends."

I raise a brow at him. "Does she know that?"

Easton shrugs. When I continue to stare him down, he lets out a groan.

"Look, I don't do anything to lead her on," he insists, slumping back in the chair. "I've even told her I just want to be friends, and she says she's cool with it, so..." Another shrug.

"She may say that, but I think she likes you," I tell him.

"I know, but I don't feel the same way about her. She's a good friend, though. Always has been." He combs his fingers through his hair and sighs. "I have a feeling that one day I'm going to lose her as a friend when she realizes I won't ever reciprocate her feelings. And that just makes me sad."

"Maybe she'll eventually move on and then you guys can be friends," I suggest. "Or maybe one day you'll end up falling in love with her."

He shakes his head. "Nah, I don't think that'll ever happen."

"You never know."

"Maybe I do, though..." He trails off as the bell rings and the teacher walks into the classroom.

I can't help wondering what he meant, like maybe somehow he knows what the future holds for him. In this new world I've been thrown into, anything seems possible.

MY FIRST TWO CLASSES AREN'T TOO TERRIBLE, but third period I end up having alone and it sucks. A lot of creatures stare at me, even through class. Even the human students stare like I've sprouted a unicorn horn out of my ass or something. At one point, I actually glance at my ass to make sure nothing is poking out of it.

As third period ends and no one says a damn word to me, I realize that people here aren't friendly. Luckily, Foster meets up with me to walk me to fourth period.

"I don't think anyone likes me very much," I remark as we walk through the hall, getting stared at. "No one but you or Easton has said a word to me."

"Humans here are just like that with new students," Foster explains. "I think mostly because they're waiting to see if you're going to end up hanging with the popular, snobby side of the school or not."

"The popular side of school?"

He leans in and whispers, "There's a divide in our school, between the elemental protectors and humans. The elemental protectors created the divide mainly because we risk our powers being discovered if we spend too much time around humans. But anyway, that divide somehow became a label. And because you're spending time with Easton and me, it means you probably got labeled as being part of the snobby, popular side."

"But then, why are no elemental protectors talking to me?"

"Some will eventually. But even our kind is cautious around Easton and me because of our last name."

"Because you're so powerful?"

"Well, that and the Everettsons have a reputation," he explains. "Mostly because of Porter. But all of us have done stuff that makes creatures cautious around us."

"Like what?" I ask, intrigued.

"Well, one time, Porter froze the whole cafeteria over on purpose." He pauses, considering something. "And Easton once flooded the school just so school had to be canceled and he could go to a concert in Elemental."

"And what about you?"

His lips quirk. "What about me?"

"Have you done anything rebellious?"

"Not on purpose, but only because I have to be more careful with my powers."

"That makes sense." I pause. "I'm surprised you guys trusted me enough to come to this school. I mean, aren't you worried I won't be able to keep my powers hidden?"

A hint of a smile graces his lips. "Sky, you spent almost eighteen years with no one knowing what you are. And if something happens and you do slip up, my parents are great at manipulating the situation. Plus, Easton and I are here to help."

Help. The word is so foreign, but I think I might really like it.

I glance down at my schedule to see which class we're heading to. Then I make a face.

"P.E.? Yuck. I seriously hoped they didn't have this class here."

"At least we have it together," he reminds me. "Easton's in it, too. And just a warning, he's super competitive, especially in dodge ball, which we play all the time." He rolls his eyes at that. "Although, I think if you smiled at him, he might go easy on you." He tosses me a teasing grin.

I roll my eyes. "I don't want him to go easy on me. I want him to play fair so, when I hit him in the face with the ball, it'll be that much more gratifying."

He chuckles, his eyes shimmering. "So, you're competitive?"

"Only in dodge ball," I say with a straight face.

He shakes his head, his grin bright and shiny and too alluring. Seriously, I can't stop staring at it.

As we slow to a stop in front of the locker rooms, his smile dims a bit.

"We have to go into separate locker rooms." He wrestles back a grin. "Unfortunately."

I roll my eyes again, but a smile tickles at my lips. But the smile is fleeting as a girl walks by and elbows me in the back. I'm not sure if it's on purpose or not, but my guard instantly goes up.

Foster must notice, too, because he frowns at the girl as she saunters into the locker room.

Frowning, he redirects his attention back to me. "If anyone bothers you in there, just send the feeling down the link."

"Why? If I do, are you going to run in there and save me?"

"Um, yeah," he replies shamelessly.

"What a brave bodyguard you are," I joke, trying to drag out my time with him. "Do you know how dangerous the girls' locker room is?"

Smiling, he nudges me toward the door. "Hurry up and get your pretty ass dressed. I'll see you in the gym."

He waits for me to open the door before he starts off toward the door to the boys' locker room.

Mustering up all the courage I have, I enter the locker room, which has lockers, along with a few bathroom stalls. At least a dozen girls are already in there and some of them glance in my direction, including a girl with blonde hair and golden eyes.

"Who is she?" she asks her friend, the girl who elbowed me in the hallway. Her eyes spark with intrigue as her golden eyes assess me.

"That's the girl Brody was telling you about, Sof," the girl replies, smirking at me.

Sofie's nostrils flare, smoke funneling out of them. "*She's* the girl Foster was holding hands with?" Her gaze drags up and down me in disdain. "Yuck. What the hell is he thinking?"

Lovely. Apparently, even mean girls exist amongst the inhuman.

Ignoring her, I head to change in one of the stalls.

As I pass them, her friend leans in and whispers something to Sofie. The grin on Sofie's face makes my stomach ravel into knots, but I maintain her gaze, letting her know I'm not afraid—well, sort of—before stepping into a stall.

Sometimes, I hate being quiet. I really do. If I were Nina, I'd have told the girl off. I've often wondered if it'd be easier to be blunt and bold as Nina. But unfortunately, it's not in my DNA.

I used to wonder why. Both my parents are pretty outspoken people. Well, toward their friends and strangers. They honestly never said much to me, except for standard conversation. Sometimes we'd go days without speaking to each other. I used to think that was normal and that it was a good thing that no one bothered me or tried to be a part of my life. I don't know, though, because over the last few days, I think maybe my opinion has changed, that it might be better having people in my life who care about me. That it's nice to know that if I did need help, I can send for it down the link, and Foster will run in here to help me. That I don't have to deal with everything alone.

I take my time changing to avoid running into Sofie and her friend, so when I finally exit the stall, the locker room is empty.

Perfect. Maybe I won't have to cross paths with anyone until I get to the gym.

That thought is short-lived, though, as Brody emerges from behind a row of lockers.

Panic storms through me and clouds appear over the ceiling. Brody doesn't notice, though, as he grins and stalks toward me.

I skitter to the side and swing around to the other side of the lockers, but he cuts me off, jogging around to the other end and blocking my path to the door.

"Relax, I'm not going to hurt you," he says, but the flames blazing in his hands suggest otherwise. "I just need to borrow you for a bit."

"Yeah, that sounds reassuring," I spit, backing away from him.

"Aw ... She does speak." His golden gaze fixes on me as he ambles toward me, unaware of the storm brewing above us.

As the clouds covering the ceiling thicken, it'll only be a slamming heartbeat more before it starts to rain. I need to settle down before he figures out what I am. At least, I should do that, but as he lunges for me, I consider releasing my power on him, letting lightning strike him where he stands. I may very well have if a guy didn't appear behind me and grab my arms.

The chill of his hands reveals he has to be an ice elemental protector.

"Let me go—"

Ice glazes through my veins. Ice not created by me.

My body temperature rapidly plunges, my skin tinting blue, and the room around me spins.

"What did you do ...?" I stagger to the side, and the fingers wrapped around my arm constrict, fingernails piercing into my skin.

"Hypothermia," Brody explains with a pleased grin. "It's a neat, little trick, isn't it?"

I glare at him as I dig deep inside myself for my powers, but everything is quiet. Too quiet. Even the clouds have evaporated.

"Put her in the basement," Brody says, looking to the side of me.

I turn my head, and my heart nearly stops.

Standing beside me is a taller guy with dark hair and the darkest eyes I've ever seen.

Elemental protector of darkness.

He grins at me, a contorted smile shadowing his lips. "My pleasure."

"W-what's i-in th-the b-basement?" I chatter out as my body grows heavy.

A wicked grin curls at Brody's lips. "It's where they keep the darkness room. It's meant for experienced elemental protectors, so it should be fun to see how it all turns out for you. Or, well, it'll be fun to see Foster get crushed when you don't make it out."

I growl at him as I stumble forward, wanting to throttle him, when another blast of cold, dark, painful madness hits me and drowns me in darkness.

Drowns me in evil.

And I feel as though I may be trapped here forever.

CHAPTER 7

I'M FREEZING AND MY HEAD FEELS LIKE IT'S IN knots. That's the first thing I become aware of when I open my eyes again. Every limb in my body aches, and my head throbs. It's also very dark. So dark I question if I don't have my eyes open. But even after I blink a few times, darkness continues to haunt every inch of my vision. That's when reality throat punches me.

Brody. The ice. The elemental protector of darkness. The room of darkness.

I'm in the darkness room, and while I have no clue what that is, considering darkness is supposed to be evil ...

As adrenaline soars through me, I wait for lightning to light up the room, but that never happens. Instead, the darkness thickens around me.

"Don't panic. You're not in here alone." Brody's voice floats through the darkness.

I push up on my hands and knees and strain my eyes to see past the darkness.

"You don't need to be nervous." This time his breath touches my ear. "I just want to play for a bit."

I swing my arm back, my fist colliding with his stomach. He grunts in pain, but quickly recovers, grabbing a fistful of my hair.

"Fight all you want, but the only way out of this room is if my friend Anders lets you out, and he's not going to do that. In fact, he's standing outside, waiting for me to get done with you, and then he's going to unleash darkness on you full force."

I'm guessing Anders is the elemental protector of darkness who helped Brody put me in here. Not that it matters right now. All that does is getting the hell out of here.

Send help down the link. Now, Sky!

The thing is, I'm not sure how the link fully works, but I do my best to allow the fear pulsating through me to current down the invisible link that connects me to all the Everettson brothers—

I gasp as Brody tugs harder on my hair, forcing me to turn over. I instinctively bring my knee up and collide it with his stomach. He curses then climbs on top of me.

"Don't worry," he whispers, pinning me down to the floor. "I'll make it quick."

I scream, reaching up to hit him, but he captures my wrists and pins my arms down. Then he forces his lips roughly on mine.

Panic slashes through me, and I again attempt to channel my powers, but only silence whispers through my body.

He kisses me harder, slipping his tongue into my mouth. I bite down on it. Instead of pulling away, though, he digs his fingernails into my wrists and bites down on my lip until blood pools out. I whimper in pain, and he chuckles, pressing his lips to mine again.

Why isn't my kiss making him pass out like Grey? Is it because my powers aren't working right now? Why aren't they working?

Both fueled by rage and panic, I dig deeper. For the first time ever, I beg my powers to surface, to blast through the air, to hurt Brody—

One second, Brody is pushing me down to the ground, and the next, he's tipping over and off me.

I let out a shaky breath as I hurriedly sit up, rubbing my aching wrists and trying to see through the darkness, see what happened to him. But everything is silent. Too silent.

"Look at you. A scared, little lamb," a voice whispers in my ear. Not Brody's voice either. No, this voice is a purr, a whisper of evil. *Darkness.* "Don't be frightened, little one. Master will be so pleased to hear that you're here."

Swoosh.

Something zips past my face and laughs.

"Of course, I can have a little fun first before I tell him." It laughs in my ear. "Did you know that darkness can cause insanity, usually to those who are weak-minded? Shall we find out just how strong you are?"

"Leave me alone," I bite out, rising to my feet.

Without being able to see, my equilibrium is off, my balance shaky. And with my powers muted, I can't do much but stumble around helplessly.

"Oh, I will soon enough, but what awaits for you when I do is going to make what happens next look like the fun part."

As I part my lips to scream, a puff of air hits me

in the chest and the coldness in my body expands, deepens, seeping into my mind and painting horrible memories I've never truly let myself fixate on. Of me as a young child, of being left alone all the time, how lonely I felt. The lack of love in my parents' eyes when they looked at me, as if they wished I hadn't been born. Of the one time I overheard them whispering about how much they wished they didn't have to take care of me. That I was a burden.

Tears fill my eyes as the memories shift into images I've never seen. Of my parents packing their bags and sneaking out of the house late at night. Of them leaving me behind as they take off to a new life.

A new life without me.

"Leave me alone!" I cry out, throwing my hands over my ears, the blood from my injured lip dripping down my chin.

"Why? Don't you want to see the truth?" Its cackle echoes around me.

"No!" I scream.

It laughs, the images shifting to all the times I was teased at school. Of when I was humiliated. Of the years I spent keeping my ability a secret. Of the fear I felt, the loneliness, even when I was around my friends.

Over and over again, the images play out until I collapse to my knees and curl up into a ball. Power sparks inside me, but doesn't lash out into the room. It stays within me, building inside my body, the pain and heat so potent I swear I'm going to die.

"Please make it stop," I beg, my brain aching from emotional overload. "Please."

But it only laughs and plays it all over again. "Stop? Why would I ever stop?" But then, contradicting its words, it says, "You're ... Oh, my gods. I need to somehow tell the master of darkness what you are and the condition you're in."

I'M UNSURE HOW LONG I LIE ON THE FLOOR, but at some point, I reach a sort of catatonic state.

I should be afraid. Instead, I feel a drop of relief that at least the images have stopped.

"Sky?" a voice cuts through the darkness.

Shit. It's come back.

"Go away," I say with my hands still over my

ears and my eyes tightly shut. My chest aches, like a deep wound, my eyes hurt from the tears I shed, and my veins are sizzling from the overload of power that was trapped inside my body. "Leave me alone."

Hands cup my cheeks and warmth douses through my veins, thawing some of the cold but not the agony inside my chest.

I blink my eyes open, fearing who's found me, but relief hits me at the sight of his eyes.

"Foster," I croak hoarsely.

Lightning flashes behind the silver in his eyes as he scoops me up in his arms. I'd work up a good protest, but my body feels like lead, heavy and fatigued.

"Who did this to you?" he whispers as he carries me from the darkness room and into the lighted hallway.

People are loitering around, watching us, all their eyes a vibrant shade of either lavender, silver, gold, or green, which means I must be in the elemental's building.

"It was ... It was Brody and a couple of his friends," I croak out, loathing how feeble I sound. I lower my voice and whisper, "Foster, I think Brody's still in that room. He tried to kiss me, and I

..." I trail off as guilt, fear, and anger rupture through me.

Guilt that I may have hurt someone. Fear that everyone will find out what I am if they discover Brody passed out on the floor. And anger that, deep down, I know what that fucker was going to do to me if kissing me hadn't knocked him out.

Maybe it makes me sick and twisted, but part of me is glad he's lying on the floor in the dark, most likely poisoned from the kisses he stole from me.

Foster glances down at me, the lightning in his eyes illuminating behind the grey as he notes my bloody lip.

"Take her," he bites out, his heart rate thundering like an out of control storm.

I'm shifted into Easton's arms. He swallows audibly as he stares down at me with a pained expression. I've never seen him look so upset.

"Come on; let's get you out of here," he utters, then starts down the hallway with me in his arms.

"What about Foster?" I ask, peering behind us.

"Foster will be fine," he says as he pushes out the door.

As we step outside, I look back into the hallway

one last time and catch a glimpse of Foster striding back into the room of darkness, with his fists balled at his sides, looking as if he's about to commit murder.

Frowning, I look away. I feel like shit, broken and dirty inside. Not to mention pathetic. I mean, it's my first day at a new school and I'm being carried out like a damsel in distress. Not a good way to start things off. I want to get down and walk with my head held high, but I can barely keep my eyes open.

Fighting to stay awake, I direct my attention back to Easton. He has a grim look on his face as he glances up at the stormy sky.

When I was in that room, I couldn't channel my powers outside of my body. Even now, the sky is strangely quiet. I wonder why. If it was from the cold Brody's friend instilled in my body or something else.

"Where was I?" I ask. "I mean, what was that room I was in?"

His gaze drops to me. "That's the room they use to train elemental protectors to fight darkness. While a creature is in there, their powers are restrained within their bodies, because the training is supposed to be a mental thing, since darkness mostly attacks mentally."

I swallow the lumped in my throat. "It showed me horrible things ... Some, I'm not sure if they were true or not, but they were still horrible."

"I'm sorry you had to go through that," he says as we reach the car. "And I'm sorry we allowed it to happen ... Foster and I could feel your fear, but we had no idea where you were because of the restraint on your power ... But we could still feel it... that heat and overwhelming ..." He pauses, taking a breath. "Nothing like that will ever happen again. We fucked up this time, but I swear we'll keep a better eye on you from now on."

I'm not naïve enough to believe they can watch me twenty-four seven. And honestly, I don't want them to. What I want is to be able to handle those situations myself. Hopefully, in time, after I've learned more about my powers, I can do just that.

In fact, I think I'll make it a goal—to become the most badass elemental enchanter who's ever lived, one no one will ever mess with. That way, I can protect myself. With what I am, I really do need to.

"East," I whisper tiredly. "I think I may have really hurt Brody ... He kissed me, and then he tipped over and ... He was really silent."

His expression turns guarded. "Whatever

happened to Brody, I'm sure he deserved it. You need to remember that, okay? He tried to hurt you, so he brought this on himself."

I press my hand to my stomach as my gut ravels into tight knots. "What if I killed him?"

"You didn't."

"How can you be so sure?"

"Because it'll take a bit more than a kiss to do so, but he's probably in some pain right now."

Images pull at my mind ...

"Easton ... the darkness in that room ... the last thing it said to me was that it needed to somehow go tell its master of darkness what I am and the condition I'm in—"

The roaring of engines cut me off.

Easton turns toward two motorcycles zooming in through the gated entrance. The drivers have helmets on, but the way Easton visibly relaxes has me wondering if they're his brothers.

Two seconds later, my guess is confirmed as Easton mumbles, "Porter and Max are here... They must have felt you."

"Felt me?" I stare up at him, lost.

"Your fear through the link," he explains, adjusting me in his arms.

"Oh..." My words get smothered by the loudness of the engines as the motorcycles pull up and park beside us.

The engines shut off, then the drivers climb off and remove their helmets.

"What the fuck happened?" Max tosses his helmet onto the seat of his motorcycle, then rakes his fingers through his dark hair, the strands somehow falling perfectly into place. "We felt something down the link and I..." He massages the center of his chest, as if his heart deeply aches.

Easton's chest rises and crashes as he releases an unsteady exhale. "This guy Brody has been holding a grudge against Foster for a while, and when he saw Foster with Sky, he decided to get back at Foster by... by locking Sky in the room of darkness." He shakes his head, the muscle in his jaw pulsating. "Then he tried to kiss her and... fuck. This is so messed up."

Max pales as he looks down at me. "Are you okay?"

I nod, even though I'm not sure I am. "Yeah... I think so..." A yawn escapes me. "I'm just a bit tired."

"Look, can you guys take her home?" Easton asks his brothers. "I think I need to go find Foster and make sure he doesn't do anything stupid."

"You probably should. I can feel a lot of anger through the link right now," Max mutters, stepping toward East. "Give her to me. Porter and I will take her home in the car. Hunter's on his way too. I think he's taking a portal, though, so if he gets here in time, we'll have him ride home with us. You and Foster can drive those home." He nods at the motorcycles then takes me from Easton's arms.

"I can walk," I say with wavering confidence as I move to climb out of his arms.

But Max only holds me tighter against his chest. "Stay still and let me carry you."

My lips part in a protest, but Porter cuts me off as he steps closer to Max and I and leans over me.

"Honey, you can barely keep your eyes open." His head angles to his side, then he reaches out and traces his fingers underneath my eyes. "You should try to go to sleep. Let your power rest for a bit."

I want to stay awake, but dreamland tugs at my mind, and hastily pulls me under.

CHAPTER 8

WHEN I OPEN MY EYES AGAIN, I'M LYING IN MY
bed and darkness has settled across the sky outside.

Even with all the sleep, I feel groggy as I sit up
and stretch my arms out. On a positive note, a lamp
has been left on, so I'm not completely in the dark.
But my head is also buzzing with confusion and
my stomach is rumbling with hunger.

As I climb out of bed to go find something to
eat, my mind races with questions.

Before I walk out of the room, I check my
reflection in the mirror to see if anything that
happened to me today did any physical damage. I
instantly cringe at how swollen my lip is and the
dried blood left over from where Brody bit me.

Rage simmers underneath my skin, and the sky

outside reacts, lightning reflecting across the darkness. I take a few breaths to steady my rage then step out of my room.

The house is silent as I make my way down the hallway and toward the stairs, not even Kash the faerie is shrieking. I begin to question if anyone is home, but when I walk into the kitchen, Foster's standing near the kitchen island, cupping the side of his face with his hand.

His gaze collides with mine as I enter the room, his eyes back to the striking shade of lightning-blue.

"Hey," he greets me with a hesitant smile. "How are you feeling?" He shakes his head. "Sorry, that's a dumb fucking question, isn't it?"

"No, it really isn't." I pad over to him and lean against the counter. "I'm fine for the most part, but I'm really confused how I got here. The last thing I can remember Porter, Hunter, and Max putting me in the car."

"They brought you home after that," he explains, searching my eyes worriedly. "How are you feeling about the all stuff that happened? About Brody and being in that room?"

I smash my lips together, unsure if I want to, or even can, answer him.

If I let myself think about what happened in that room, I can almost feel Brody's lips against mine and feel the pain of seeing the images that darkness showed me. Particularly the ones of my parents leaving me. Could that be true? Could they have left me? Did they ever care about me?

Does anyone care about me?

"I'm not sure how I feel..." I admit. "Did you ...?" I struggle to get the words out. "Did you find Brody in that room?"

He nods. "I did."

"Was he ...? Was he okay?"

Foster works his jaw from side to side. "He was okay until I got ahold of him."

My stomach clenches. "What did you do?"

"Nothing he didn't deserve," Foster bites out. "Not after what he did to you ... And locking you in that fucking room ..." An uneven exhale eases from his lips. Then, with his free hand, he brushes his finger lightly across my bottom lip, his face a portrait of pain. With each stroke of his finger, I swear the imprint of Brody's lips against mine fades.

"Did ...? Did Easton tell you what darkness said to me in that room?" I can barely utter the words, too distracted by how calm his touch is making me feel. "About knowing what I am and the condition I'm in?"

He nods, tracing his fingers along my hairline and pushing my hair back from my eyes. "I sent a message to my parents about it. I'm not sure if the darkness in that room can actually escape and contact the elemental god of darkness or if it was just trying to screw with you, but they're going to try to find out. Until then, we're going to lay low and stay at the house, okay?"

"But what did darkness mean when it said, the condition I'm in?"

"I'm not sure. But my best guess is you being locked in that room and that it was draining your powers from you."

I take a subtle breath as I attempt to process everything he just told me. How my lips hurt Brody. How my powers seeped into the Everettson brothers.

I'm such a risk. Why would anyone ever want to be around me? Not that the Everettsons have a choice in the matter, I guess. Well, unless their parents decide to kick my ass to the curb.

"So, no more school for now?" I attempt to focus on something else instead of my sudden burst of self-loathing.

He nods. "Not until my mom finds out more about the room of darkness."

"What if they do find out it warned the god of darkness?" Not that I'm saddened by the fact that I get a few days off from having to go to that school again. In fact, I'm grateful I don't have to go back yet.

Honestly, I wish I never had to return.

"We'll figure that out when the time comes. If nothing else, we can attend another school. We just need to make sure you're well protected and that darkness doesn't know where you are. Here, you're pretty damn safe. There're enough protection spells around our house."

"That's good." I work to bottle back the fear creeping through me, but a bit oozes through, making the light bulbs flicker on and off. "So, there're more schools for elementals on earth?"

His gaze flits from the flickering light bulbs to me. "They're a ways away, but yeah." He draws a path with his fingertip down the side of my face to my jawline, his eyes crammed with puzzling guilt. "I'm so sorry for letting that happen to you. What happened to you while you were in that room was probably awful, and I ... I wish ... I'm so sorry. I promised you'd be safe, and I failed you."

"You didn't fail me." I'm taken aback by the guilt in his voice. "Stuff like that happened to me all the time in my normal school. Well, not that I was ever locked in a room of darkness, but one time, some guys locked me in the janitor's closet. But I'm sure they would've locked me in a room of darkness if we had one at our school."

"What happened today should've never happened. And what happened in your past should've never happened either. You never should've had to go through any of what you did ... Brody ..." His fingers twitch and his whole body tightens. "He only did it to get back at me. If I'd just been nice when I turned Sofie down, none of this would've happened."

"I'm not so sure about that. I briefly met Sofie and her friend, who apparently saw me holding your hand at school—that's what she was upset about. And besides, if you had to reject her several times, she should've taken the hint long before she did."

"Maybe." He studies me, sketching his fingers along my hairline then my jaw. "What all did they do to you? Brody and his lackeys ... I know you said Brody kissed you, but ..." He swallows, the ground shaking with whatever he's feeling inside.

I shrug, but a foul taste burns at my tongue. "Brody made his friend drop my body temperature to a hypothermic level, and then his other friend blasted me with darkness. After that, I blacked out and woke up in that room. Brody was there, and he ... well, he tried to kiss me, and then bit my lip when I bit his tongue." My voice quivers, and I swiftly clear my throat. "But, yeah, anyway, he didn't get very far before he passed out." But, did he even pass out? I never did see him afterward ...

Remorse pours from Foster's lightning-blue gaze. "I'm so fucking sorry, but I promise, that if we return to the academy, you won't have to worry about Brody or his friends again. From now on, you're going to feel safe."

The way he says I'll never have to worry about being hurt by Brody again leaves me wondering if he hasn't told me the full story. That maybe...

"Did I ...? Did my kiss kill Brody?" I blurt out.

Foster swiftly shakes his head. "No, he just passed out. I swear."

Relief trickles through me, but rapidly dissipates. "Did you kill him?"

"As much as I wanted to, no, I didn't. When he woke up, I did get a few good punches in and blasted water through his body. Then someone broke up the fight. And since Brody was already on probation, he got kicked out of school." He sweeps his knuckles across my cheek, watching in fascination as my eyelashes flutter. "Him and his friends who locked you in that room are never allowed on school grounds again."

"What about Sofie?"

"With a bit of practice, you'll be able to handle Sofie if you need to. Her powers are weak."

"I don't even know how to use my powers properly. Today more than proves that."

"What happened today wasn't your fault. And you'll learn how to control your powers in time. My brothers and I will make sure of that. In fact, we should probably start as soon as possible." He lowers his hand from his cheek, revealing a gnarly bruise forming on his skin.

"Holy shit, did Brody do that to you?"

He gives a dismissive shrug. "It's just a little bruise. Brody ended up way worse. He's lucky I was smart enough to control most of my powers or his ass might have been fried."

I place my hand on his cheek, and light skims across my fingers and along the bruise. "Why's your skin so cold?"

He lifts the hand he'd been holding against his

cheek and lines his palm against the side of my neck. I flinch as a chill bites my flesh and let out a squeal.

"I used my ice power to make an ice pack." He withdraws his hand with a trace of a grin on his face.

Remembering the goal I made to myself earlier, I ask, "Can you show me how to do that?"

"Sure." He sets his hand on top of mine, trapping my palm against his cheek. "Just think about coldness seeping through your veins and channel it toward your hand. It also helps to visualize it."

I do what he says, and only a handful of seconds later, my hand is as cold as an ice pack.

He smiles. "You catch on to everything so easily. It makes me wonder how powerful you're going to be."

His compliment makes me blush, but weirdly, it doesn't make the ice in my hand melt.

"Don't be embarrassed about being powerful. It's a good thing."

"I'm not embarrassed about that. It's just ..." *Stupid flushing cheeks.* "I just don't do well with compliments ... I'm not used to them."

"I have no idea how that's possible." His gaze searches my face. Then he steps forward, backing me up against the counter. "You're so gorgeous, smart, powerful, funny, and brave. How has no one ever told you that?"

"Because I'm not any of those things, and I'm definitely not brave. I mean, I cried when I was in the darkness room, for hell's sake. That's not bravery."

He looks at me solemnly. "That room is made for experienced elemental protectors who've had years and years of practice fighting against evil. The fact that you made it out of there and are standing here talking to me, completely sane, proves how brave and powerful you are."

"Maybe I'm not sane right now," I quip, trying to lighten the mood before my powers start to surface.

His expression is serious as he rests a hand on my hip. "You're impressive. That's what you are."

His gaze zeroes in on my lips. I remain motionless, more conflicted than I was earlier when he tried to kiss me. I'm not even sure why, or what I want. Maybe it's the stress of the day. Or maybe it's because the more time we spend together, the more connected and at ease I feel with him.

But, do I really want him to kiss me? Does he really want to kiss me? Especially after everything that happened? After Brody just forced a kiss on me?

His lips never touch mine, though. Instead, he rests his forehead against mine. He doesn't say anything, just breathes in and out with his hands on my hips. I think I might like him a bit in this moment, for not trying to kiss me when I'm not sure if I'm ready for it.

As we settle into silence, his power currents into me, warm and calming, and I'm pretty sure some of mine whisks into him.

While I've never actually, *really* kissed anyone, I wonder if it's overrated, because there's no way it could feel better than this ... than our powers and this ... calm he's putting inside me.

"You feel so good," he whispers, his breath tickling my cheeks. "Like everything and nothing at the same time."

I understand what he means. While his touch and power bring a calmness to me, it also pours the most wonderful energy inside me.

"Sky," he whispers. "When I felt how scared you were when you were put in that room ... and I couldn't find you ... I just ... Dammit." He tenses.

My eyes pop open—I hadn't even been aware I

closed them—as he pushes away from me and glares at something over my shoulder.

When I twist around, Easton is leaning against the doorframe with his arms crossed and smile playing at his lips.

"I hate to break up this little moment—and yes, that's sarcasm—because good gods, you two need to fuck before the rest of us spontaneously combust from your sexual tension." He grins at me and I glare in returning. His grin broadens then he focuses on Foster. "Mom's about to send a message through a secured magical signal and wants you guys to be present for it."

I angle my head to the side. "What's a secured magical signal?"

"It's ..." Foster starts then pauses. "Well, it's easier to see it than try to explain it."

Okay, now I'm a bit curious. "For how long is your mom going to be gone?"

"We're not sure yet," Foster says. "And actually, everyone is gone right now. You, Easton, and me are the only ones here."

"Porter, Hunter, and Max left already?" I ask.

He nods, his face a mask of guardedness. "Right after they dropped you off, they got called on a job. So did Holden."

"Where are your parents?" I ask.

"On missions," Foster says. "Well, my dad is on a personal mission in Shimmerland, the world of faeries. He's looking for some faerie dust so he can concoct a potion that'll hopefully erase Kash's memory."

"So he won't remember what we are?"

"Yep," Easton is the one to answer. "And then we can kick his ass out of the house."

"He was really quiet when I walked by the room just barely," I tell them. "I thought maybe he was gone."

"Nah, he's still there. He probably just screamed himself to sleep," Easton explains. "Thank the gods. He screams are more high-pitched than a whining unicorn."

My jaw drops. "*Unicorns* exist."

"They do." Easton smirks at me. "Maybe if you're *really* nice to me, I'll show you one some-day." When I roll my eyes, he grins then looks back at Foster. "Just an FYI. Everyone's going to be gone for a few days."

Foster slips his fingers through mine. "When is Mom sending the message?"

"In like three seconds—"

Poof.

A lavender cloud of smoke puffs up in the center of the kitchen, hovering just above the kitchen island and taking the form of Emaline.

"Oh, good. You're all here." Her cloudy eyes glance at the three of us then settle on me. "I just wanted to check in and see how everyone's doing, especially you, Sky. I heard what happened, and I feel awful. After we spent so much time assuring you that everything would be all right, this happens. Plus, that whole ordeal with darkness ..." She shakes her head. "We're currently working on finding out if the darkness in that room can send messages to the outside world. But I promise that you're safe with Easton and Foster. They won't let anything happen to you. I don't want you to be afraid."

"I'm fine," I try to reassure her, even though I'm not sure I am

She gapes at me in disbelief, smoke twirling around her. "I want to talk more about it when I get back, but right now, I wanted to let you know that nothing like that will happen again. If you go back to that school, we'll make sure no one harms you again." She waits for me to nod then directs her attention to Foster and Easton.

"I wanted to let you two know that, as of this

morning, the council has gone silent. Between that and what happened at the school, you're all on high alert until we find out more about what's going on. You are to be guarded by protection spells at all times and, for now, you're just going to have to hang out in the house."

"No one knows what the silence from the council is over?" Easton asks, resting his arms on the counter.

She shakes her head, her hair moving like wisps behind her. "Your father's looking into it. I'm still working on … something else."

Her vagueness sends warning flags popping up everywhere.

She's being discreet, but about what?

"Look, I have to go. I'm in the middle of something really important, but I'll check in tomorrow morning." Apprehension floods her features as she gives a pressing look at her sons. "If anything happens, you know what to do."

Easton and Foster nod, and then just as quickly as she materialized, she evaporates into a cloud of smoke.

"That was … weird," I state, staring at the traces of smoke lingering in the air. "And, why did she seem so worried about the council going quiet?"

Foster shares a troubled look with Easton then turns to me. "Because the last time they went quiet and didn't communicate with anyone was when the gods and goddesses died."

A nagging pain starts to prod at my chest. "Do you think someone else has died?"

"I really have no idea," he says.

So then, why does he look so worried?

EVERYONE REMAINS FAIRLY QUIET AFTER THAT.

Eventually, I make myself something to eat then head back to bed to get some rest. Even though I've been sleeping for most of the day, I feel drained. When I tell Foster this, he explains that being in the room of darkness drained a lot of my energy. But he assures me that, with how powerful I am, I should feel replenished in the morning after a full night's rest. The problem is, I'm terrified to go to sleep, that darkness will visit me in my nightmares.

"Are you okay?" Foster asks as we stop in front

of my bedroom door. "You've been really quiet since my mom sent her message."

"I don't know," I answer honestly. "It just feels like you guys are keeping some stuff from me. Not that I blame you. I know you don't know me very well. But it's weird feeling like such an outsider all the time."

"It's not that." He folds his arms across his chest and shifts his weight. "We just don't talk a lot about the missions my parents go on. At least, not the full details. It's not allowed."

"Oh, okay." I turn to go into my room, unsure if I'm buying what he said.

As soon as my gaze lands on the darkness covering the sky outside my window, I pause.

Foster moves up behind me. "What is it?"

"It's nothing." I give a shrug. "I'm just nervous about going to sleep and maybe having nightmares about darkness." I feel like a wimp. "It says such creepy-ass things to me. And the images I saw in the room ..."

Seriously, though, where is my badassery? I need to get over this. So, maybe my mom and dad did leave me? Who cares? I should be tougher than this. And it's not like I haven't been on my own before. Still, knowing they maybe just me left hurts like a bitch.

"Can I ask you something? It's about the room of darkness and whether the stuff it showed me was real."

Foster hesitates. "Darkness has the ability to read creature's fears, so what it showed you may have held a bit of truth, but it's also spun with a web of exaggeration, if that makes sense."

I wrap my arms around myself. "It showed my parents leaving me."

"Even if that held any truth to it, it's your parents' loss. Not yours." He loops his arms around my waist, his movements a bit fumbling, revealing he's nervousness. "You're an amazing creature, and anyone who gets you in their life is very lucky. We all knew that from the moment we met you. You were nice, even though we were acting like assholes. And then you said a few smartass remarks and that made us like you even more."

"It sure didn't seem like you guys liked me."

"Trust me; we're good at wearing masks, but the link doesn't lie."

Am I pathetic for liking what he said about them liking me? Is it bad to want to be part of someone else's life and for them to want you to be?

"Do you want me to lie beside you while you fall asleep?" he asks with a nervous edge in his tone. "I can help you try to control the nightmares. My mom used to do it for me when I was little. It helped sometimes."

When I was younger, I used to have nightmares. My mom and dad would always get mad at me when I tried to sneak into their room and sleep on the floor. I used to wished that someone would comfort me or at least tell me everything will be okay. Maybe even give me a hug.

Whether it makes me weak or not, I nod. "Yeah, okay. That sounds ..." *Wonderful*, I want to say, but then I mentally kick my own ass and settle on, "good."

"Are you sure ...? You sound hesitant."

I nod. "Yep, I'm sure." I think.

He moves back. "I'll give you a couple of minutes to change."

Nodding, I step into my room and shut the door. Then I put on a pair of plaid pajama shorts and a tank top, pull my hair into a messy bun, and grab my phone to text Nina and Gage, deciding I need some BFF time after the crappy day I've had.

Me: So, maybe they're not as bad as I thought ...

Nina: Ha! I knew you'd fall for one of them? The question is: which one?

Me: None. I just decided they're not as bad as I thought.

Nina: Liar. I bet it's the one from the parking lot, right?

Gage: The one who treated her like shit?

Me: I didn't fall for any of them ... But Foster, the guy from the parking lot, he's not as bad anymore. In fact, he's pretty nice.

Nina: Blah. Nice is sooo boring.

Gage: You only think that because you love drama.

Nina: Ha! Like you don't.

Gage: Whatever. You're way worse than me.

Me: Both of you are terrible if you ask me.

Nina: Whatever. You both suck. Just kidding. I love you guys.

Me: I love you guys, too. I mean that. I really do.

Gage: Okay, now you got me worried. What's up with the mushiness?

Me: It's nothing. I just had a rough day.

A rough day where I realized that, before I moved here, the two of them were the only stable people in my life. Not that they're stable in the head or anything like that. But, as friends, they've been pretty solid.

Nina: You want us to come visit? You seem sad. And while we're there, we can see for ourselves if this Foster dude is really worthy of you.

I wish I could see them, wish it was okay, but with everything going on and us being on lockdown, it's safer if they're not around.

Me: I have school for the next couple of weeks, but we for sure need to get together soon and hang out.

But I have to wonder if I'll be able to or if, the deeper I fall into this world, the more distance I'll have to put between us.

I don't have too much time to stress out over those questions, though, because someone knocks on the door. I send Nina and Gage a quick text saying I have to go then put my phone away, get up, and answer the door.

Foster is standing on the other side, and his gaze skims up and down me as he enters my bedroom. "You ready for bed?"

"Nah, I just put on my pajamas for fun," I joke. "Thought I'd make a new fashion statement. In fact, I think I should wear this to school."

"Such a smartass." Shaking his head and suppressing a grin, he crosses the room and flops down on the bed.

He's wearing a pair of plaid pajama bottoms and a black T-shirt, but as he tucks his arms behind his head, his shirt rides up and I get a glimpse of his lean abs. Then I roll my eyes at myself for gawking at him and lie down beside him, keeping a bit of distance between us, despite how much I want to snuggle up with him and feel at ease. It would be a stupid move, and I'd be stupid for doing it.

"You want the lights on or off?" Foster asks, rotating onto his side.

I also roll onto my side to face him. "Can we keep the lamp on?"

He nods then scoots closer, tracing his hand up and down my arm.

Up ...

And down …

Why is he really here? What does he really want from me?

Finally, the unknown becomes too much. Later, I might blame what I say next on exhaustion, but right now, I'm too tired to care.

"Do you really like me?" I ask the question that's been bugging me since I found out what it really means to be an elemental enchanter. "Or are you just acting this way because of what I am?" I mentally roll my eyes at myself. Did I seriously just ask him if he liked me, like we're in grade school or something?

His gaze relentlessly burns into mine. "I swear I'm not here with you just because of what you are."

I'm unsure if I believe him or not, but decide to just let it be for right now because I'm fucking tired. How, though, who the heck knows, since I've been sleeping almost the entire day.

Silence fills the room, but even though I'm exhausted, I can't seem to doze off.

"What was it like growing up knowing what you are?" I ask when the silence starts to drive me crazy. "Did you always attend the same school? Did you always live here?"

"I've always lived and gone to school here. Porter, Max, Holden, and Hunter were all born in Elemental, though, before the gods and goddesses started to die. But when that happened, my parents decided to move here. They didn't want to raise their family in a dying world that was plagued by darkness. As for what it was like growing up knowing what I am, it actually sucked. Not because I had powers, but because of the powers I had and knowing I was more than likely going to live a lonely life and would always have a target on my back." He shifts closer to me. "My parents and brothers have been great and everything, but it'd be nice to just once be able to live my life how I want, without having to worry about what I'm feeling inside. I also sometimes wish I could travel the worlds; just pack up and go, doing whatever I want. I might one day if I can figure out a better way to hide my identity."

"My friends and I had that plan, too—to travel after we graduated. Unfortunately, I'm starting to wonder if that's going to happen. But I'm not even sure if it ever would've happened. Even though my friends and I are close, I still always have to put up this wall between us, and that makes spending every waking moment with them complicated."

Reluctance currents off him. "If you want, you and I can find a way to hide our identities and travel the worlds together. We can just take off, see the worlds, live in different cultures."

Could I do that? Do I want to do that? What about my plan with Nina and Gage?

But everything is so different now. Knowing what I know—that my existence could put them in danger—I'm not sure I could be around them all the time.

"That sounds nice, actually," I admit, but I feel a bit guilty for bailing on my friends.

What world do I really belong in?

Who am I really?

Will I ever have the answers?

"Good." He sounds happy about the fact. "Then I'll get working on making it happen."

With that, sleep begs me to give in, and I surrender. But, as I begin to doze off, I feel his lips brush my forehead as he softly whispers, "One day, beautiful girl, I'll prove to you that I liked you way before you liked me. Then you won't have to worry about that anymore."

I want to ask him how and reprimand him for calling me beautiful, but sleep gets the best of me and, seconds later, I drift off to dreamland.

CHAPTER 9

I'M FLOATING IN A BOLT OF LIGHTNING WITH A crown on my head and an abundance of power is channeling through me.

"Feel the power inside you," someone whispers. "Do you have any idea what you are—"

My eyes pop open, my mind racing along with my pulse. And I swear I can still feel the power flowing through my body.

I shake my head as I work to get my breathing under control. What a weird ass dream? But I guess it was better than dreaming of darkness. And I guess all of my dreams have been weird since I was thrown into this strange world of elemental powers

I let out a yawn and stretch my arms above my

head. Then I move to roll out of bed, only to end up rolling straight into Foster.

He grunts as my knee collides with his gut.

"Sorry," I sputter.

I'd almost forgotten that last night I'd asked him to sleep with me. But how in the hell did we end up so close with my leg thrown over his and our heads inches apart?

"It's fine," he assures me, rubbing the spot on his stomach where I kneed him. "I'm just glad you slept okay. Or I'm assuming you did since I didn't sense you wake up at all during the night."

"Yeah, I slept great," I say. "But how did you know I slept all through the night? Unless you were awake all night, watching me sleep?" I ask with teasing accusation.

He flushes a bit. "Maybe I was." He pauses, then gives me a quick kiss on the cheek and climbs out of bed.

My heart flutters and my head spins. He just kissed me on the cheek. His lips were so soft and felt so good against my skin.

He feels so good.

"Easton messaged me a couple of minutes ago and said my mom messaged him," Foster says, stretching his arms above his head.

His shirt rides up, giving me a view of his lean abs and the lightning tattoo inking his flesh.

Stop staring at him like a perv, Sky. Get your head out of lust land.

I yank my gaze off him, relieved he hasn't noticed I was just eye fucking the hell out of his stomach muscles. "What'd she say?"

His hands fall to his sides. "That she still hasn't been able to get ahold of the headmistress, so we have to stay in the house still. But Easton and I thought maybe we could help you practice using your powers while we're stuck here."

"That sounds really great, actually." Although the idea of using my powers on purpose has me nervous. "Is it safe to do that in the house, though?"

He drags his hand over the top of his head, making strands of his hair go askew. "We'll probably stick to the pool house since there's limited things in there that we can ruin, but you practicing is more important than a few things getting broken."

Maybe he's right, but that doesn't mean I won't feel bad if I ruin something. Emaline and Gabe have been so nice to me that the last thing I want to do is set their house on fire.

"I'll make sure your powers don't get too out of hand," he adds.

"Okay, let's do it then. But, while we're at it, can you teach me how to block out what I'm feeling from flowing down the link? It's starting to really become a pain in the ass."

"Maybe it is for you, but I think some of my brothers find it amusing." When I grimace, he chuckles, his eyes crinkling around the corners. "Yeah, I can show you. Just know that the link's still there if you ever need it. You never have to be alone in this, okay?"

I nod, my heart constricting at his words. I'm not alone in this.

I'm not alone anymore.

My heart starts doing really weird things, but I shove the feelings aside, silently telling my heart to quit being a dumbass.

After Foster leaves, I get dressed, putting on a pair of black, stretchy jeans and a matching shirt. Then I pull my hair into a ponytail and head downstairs to the kitchen to make myself something to eat. When I get there, though, plates of bacon and eggs are already on the kitchen island.

"Good morning," Charlotte greets me as she wipes down the countertops with a dishrag.

"Hey." I peer around the empty kitchen. All the appliances look polished and sparkly and the air smells like bacon with a hint of lemon cleaner. "Where are Foster and Easton?"

"They haven't come down here yet." She moves on to wiping down the stove, giving me a smile from over her shoulder. "They're worse than a couple of girls when it comes to getting ready. Well, either that or my girls just got ready quickly."

"You have kids then?" I ask, plopping down onto a barstool.

She nods, tossing the dishrag down and turning to face me. "Three actually. But they're grown up now and married with their own kids."

"Where's your husband?" I wonder as I shovel up a forkful of eggs.

She frowns, agony filling her eyes, and I immediately regret my words.

"He died about a decade ago at the hand of an elemental protector of darkness, but that's becoming more and more common in Elemental." She wraps her arms around herself. "His death is part of the reason I decided to leave our world and come work for the Everettsons. My children left, too. And while I'm glad we're all okay, I long for the days when we can all live in our world safely and not have to live in hiding." She reaches across the counter and pats my hand. "Something I'm sure you understand."

"Maybe a little. At least the having to hide my powers part." I chew on a bite of eggs. "How did you end up working for the Everettsons?"

A smile touches her lips. "Gabe's parents were friends of my husband's and mine, and when they mentioned needing a housekeeper, I volunteered. They've been so good to me, and they are great creatures. They're always trying to help everyone, even if it means risking their own safety."

I nod in understanding. "They risked a lot taking me in, too."

"I know, but I know for a fact they're happy to do it. Especially Foster. That poor boy has been so lonely and sad since his grandparents passed away. I can only imagine how hard it was for him to think he lost the last of his kind." She muses over something with a small smile. "Although, he's been a lot happier the last couple of days. Not that he's ever treated me poorly. That boy has always been a sweetheart, even if he pretends otherwise to most people. Still, I can't believe what fate did to him. That the girl he liked would end up being the girl meant for him."

Her words send confusion through me since Foster has only mildly liked me for a couple of days. I open my mouth to ask her what she meant, but her gaze wanders to something over my shoulder.

"Speaking of which."

I twist around and find Foster entering the kitchen and shaking his head. His hair is damp, which probably means he just showered, and he's dressed in his usual head-to-toe black attire with leather bands and studs to match.

"I have a feeling I was just being talked about." Foster glances suspiciously from Charlotte to me.

"And your feelings are correct." Grinning, she hands him a plate of eggs and bacon.

Foster takes the plate from her. "Okay, what were you saying?"

I'm actually pretty eager to hear myself, especially to hear what she meant by *the girl he liked ending up being meant for him*. But she only gives him a smile and a wink then heads for the door.

"I'll be in my room today, working on some spells. If you need anything, let me know. And please, don't burn the house down." With that, she exits the kitchen.

I glance at Foster, trying to put together some pieces I feel like I'm missing.

"What did she say to you?" Foster asks, nervously shifting his weight.

I shrug. "I don't know. Just some stuff about her and her family and you." I wait for him to ask what she said about him, but he must not want to hear since he simply tugs on my hand and steers me out of the room.

"Come on; let's go eat our breakfast in the pool room then get our practice session started."

THE POOL HOUSE IS A MASSIVE ROOM WITH, yeah, you guessed it, a pool. There're also massive, flourishing trees that stretch toward the glass ceiling that gives an awesome view of the sky. When we first walked in, it had been mildly cloudy outside, but the more I use my powers, the stormier it gets. So far, though, nothing has been set on fire nor has it rained. I think that might be due to Foster syphoning some of my powers, though, and not because I've suddenly become a badass at using them.

"Okay, I want to try something new," Foster tells me as he lines his palms with mine again.

He's standing in front of me with his shoes off. Easton is with us, but he's lounging around in a chair beside the hot tub and texting on his phone, griping about how no one will text him back and that he's super bored.

I trap a breath in my chest, waiting for him to release some of his powers, something he's done a couple of times already, and damn, is it intense.

"I want you to try to stabilize some of my powers," he explains, tracing a finger up and down my palm. Faint, blue zaps of light emit across my skin and the air around me hums. It doesn't hurt, though. No, in fact, it's quite the opposite.

I shake my head. "I can barely stabilize my own powers, let alone yours."

"I think you can do more than you're allowing yourself," he says. "You're just too nervous to let yourself feel the full force of your powers."

"And for good reasons." I cock a brow. "Remember the grocery store fire incident I told you about?"

"I promise I won't let you start a fire. I just want you to be able to stabilize my powers so that, if anything ever happens again like with Brody and his friends, you'll be able to shove their powers out of you."

I restlessly tap my foot against the concrete. "I don't know if I can do it."

"Sky ..." Foster's tone is soft and patient. He's actually been really patient through all this, something I never would've guessed he possessed if you'd asked me a week ago. Then again, a week ago I never would've thought a bunch of people were walking around with secret powers. "I know tapping into all this power is scary, especially after you spent years trying to keep it contained, but I need you to trust me, okay?" His lightning-blue eyes spark with tiny lightning bolts. "I won't let anything happen to you."

Trust. What a strangely foreign word. A strangely foreign word that is frightening to feel.

Do I trust him?

I'm not sure. I wish I was, but I still question if he's lying to me about things.

But that doesn't mean I'm going to chicken out with this.

An exhale puffs from my lips. "All right, I'll do it."

His smile is part surprise and part awe, but he hastily collects himself. "All right, I'm going to slowly let some of my powers into you," he warns. "Don't panic, okay? And let the elements around us into you. Build your power so it can take over mine."

"I'll do my best."

He closes his eyes, his face set in deep concentration.

Despite the uneasiness stirring inside me, I find myself studying him, how beautiful he is, how...

Easton catches me gawking at his brother, and a devious grin consumes his face as he mouths, "*Busted.*"

I stick out my tongue at him, but as the taste of Foster's powers glazes inside my veins. my attention shifts from Easton to him. His icy-cold, yet somehow warm, power mixes with mine and causes a gasp to fumble from my lips.

"Collect the energy from the elements around us and mix them with yours," he whispers. Then the edges of his lips twitch. "Make my powers your little bitch."

I'd probably laugh if my heart wasn't beating like a cracked out humming bird.

Breathing shakily, I seek the energy around me, feel the air from the trees, the whisper of the rain in the clouds above, the coldness of the air, and the heat of the fire crackling in the fireplace in the living room. I sense all the elements nearby and collect them, adding them to mine, making myself become *powerful*—

Foster gasps, jerking back, his eyes flashing from lavender to green to silver to gold, and then back to lightning-blue. "Holy fuuuuck."

A burst of energy blasts out of me and sprays across the room, dusting the pool, chairs, and even Foster and Easton with little crystals in the shades of all the elements.

"I'm so sorry." I yank my hands away from his.

What did I just do?

Foster gapes at me. "Don't be. That was ... Well, that was fucking impressive."

"Fuck yeah, it was." Easton jumps to his feet, wiping the crystals off his face as he walks over to us. "Shit, she's got a lot of power. It's awesome, though. I bet she could do some crazy stuff after she's trained properly"

"Yeah, I bet she can." Foster stares at me quizzically. "The crack in her wall is growing, too. I think my powers might've done it."

Easton moves up beside me, leaning in and

assessing me with his silver eyes. "Can you see what's hidden behind it yet?"

Foster shakes his head. "Can you?"

Easton traces his finger along my collarbone. "Right here is where the crack is, right?" he asks Foster. When Foster nods, he frowns. "I can't see a damn thing either."

Foster stares at me like I'm mesmerizing, and the look makes me squirm.

"Maybe when we finally get it down, we'll figure out where the hell all her power is coming from." Foster continues to stare at me in quizzical wonderment, the crystals on his face twinkling in the light above. "You're amazing, Sky. You really are. I've never seen anything like this." His gaze descends to the crystals covering his arms and a smile graces his lips.

I flick a golden crystal off me, feeling self-conscious. "Just so you know, whatever just happened, I probably did it accidentally, so you shouldn't be too impressed."

"Accident or not, you managed to shove out any traces of Foster's powers from your body," Easton grins at me. "Do you know how badass that is?"

"It's extremely badass," Foster adds. "And rare.

In fact, I don't think I've ever heard of any other elemental being able to do that." He surveys me over. "I'd like to try it again, but only if you want to. I don't want to pressure you into doing something you're not comfortable with. But I do want to stress that the more you practice, the more powerful and safer you'll be. Plus, I think you might turn into quite the badass." He rubs at the crystals covering his arms, his touch melting them and leaving streaks of elemental colors on his flesh.

Their badass remarks are what win me over and make me want to do it again.

I hold up my palms in front of me. "All right, let's do it."

Grinning, Foster aligns his palms to mine and Easton claps his hands together.

"All right, badass girl, let's see what other awesome tricks you have hidden up your sleeve." Easton steps back, as if he expects me to do something magical.

And hey, at this point I'm kind of wondering the same thing.

Hours later, I'm beyond exhausted but

feeling pretty good. Not only did I absorb Foster's powers a few times and eliminate them from my body, but I blocked out my feelings from traveling down the link a couple of times as well. Not that I'm an expert yet. No, it'll take quite a bit of practice before I can stand in a circle amongst all the Everettsons and let them blast all their powers into me like I saw them do with Foster the day I discovered their secret. But I'm feeling more confident about my powers than I did a couple of days ago, so that's a plus.

"Is it normal to be this tired from using my powers so much?" I ask Foster as we wander down the hallway toward our bedrooms.

He flicks a few pieces of crystal off the hem of his shirt. "Yeah. Even I still get exhausted sometimes. But it's important to practice so you can go out into the worlds without having to worry about your powers getting the best of you. Plus, it's good to know you can protect yourself."

"What do you plan on doing once you graduate?" I ask through a yawn.

He stops in front of my door, his lips tugging into a half-smile. "Traveling with you. Remember?"

I slow to a stop with him. "Yeah, I remember.

But what if you'd never met me? Then what would you have done?"

His smile vanishes quicker than my heart can take its next beat. "I probably would've followed in my parents' footsteps—worked for the organization for most of my life then died alone."

His words strike me square in the chest.

"Foster ... I—"

He places his finger over my lips. "I don't want you to pity me. I know you've been just as lonely as I have. I saw it in your eyes the day I met you. But I do want you to know that you don't have to be alone anymore." He lowers his finger from my lips. "I'm so glad I met you. And I would've felt the same way I do about you now, even if you hadn't turned out to be an elemental enchanter." He gives a brief pause, his gaze dropping to my lips again. Then he turns toward his shut bedroom door.

"Wait." I call out and he pauses. "Will you ...? Will you sleep with me again?" *Face palm.*

Did I seriously just ask him to sleep with me? Sometimes, I can be so awkward.

He twists back around, his lips quirking as his gaze zones in on my flushed cheeks.

"You're so cute when you get embarrassed," he says through a soft laugh. "And yeah, I'll sleep with you, but only if you promise not to let your hands wander where they don't belong."

My cheeks flush and he grins, but looks a bit flushed himself.

"Nice one, bro." Easton snickers, appearing just down the hallway.

Great. When did he get here?

"No, not nice one bro." I throw a smirk at Easton. "Anything that you think is nice isn't nice at all. In fact, it's the opposite."

"You, lightning eyes, are becoming more and more entertaining by the day," he quips with a grin, slanting against a shut door just a ways down from my bedroom. "But what's most entertaining is when you blush."

"And on that note." I push open my bedroom door and move to step inside. "And just for the record, I wasn't blushing."

"Then why're your cheeks red?" Easton shouts out through a laugh.

"Because I'm pissed off at you." Turning around, I flip him the middle finger and grin.

He grins back, his eyes glinting wickedly.

God, he really does get off on this, doesn't he?

"Whatever. Deep down, I know you love me." A devious smile carves across his face. "Maybe not as much as you love Foster, but probably pretty close."

I narrow my eyes at him, but his smirk only turns more wicked. Then he spins on his heels and struts down the hallway with a cocky bounce in his step.

"One day, he's going to meet someone who gives him a taste of his own medicine," I murmur with a shake of my head.

"Oh, I know, and I can't wait," Foster agrees, stuffing his hands into his back pockets. "Payback is going to be a real bitch."

"Definitely." I trade a conspiratorial grin with him. "And we should make sure to tease the crap out of him when it does happen. Pay him back for all the teasing he's giving us."

"Sounds like a deal to me." He grins at me then backs toward his door. "I'm going to go get changed. I'll be right back, okay?"

I nod then hurry into my room to get changed. Once I've pulled on a pair of comfy shorts and a tank top, I climb into bed and check my messages while I wait for Foster to arrive. A frown pulls at my lips when I note there are no new messages from Nina and Gage. Not that I texted them since last night, but I've been busy. I guess they are, too.

I sigh at the screen, feeling as though we're already starting to drift apart, something I was worried about.

I'm not even sure what to do—how to stay connected to them, or if I should even try. Won't I be putting them in danger? Just how much danger am I going to be in? Will I ever feel totally safe?

Countless worries and questions haunt my mind as I wait for Foster to return.

Knock. Knock. Knock.

"Come in," I call out, setting my phone on the nightstand beside my bed.

Foster enters my room, wearing drawstring pajama bottoms and a T-shirt that has a logo that reads: *Ash East Arrow.*

"What's that?" I ask, pointing at the logo on his shirt.

"It's the band Easton ditched school to go see that one time I told you about." He stops beside my bed and picks a piece of lint off his shirt. "They're pretty popular amongst paranormals. The lead singer is actually a genie, the drummer is a cyborg, and the bassist is a faerie."

I blink stupidly at him. "Um ... Wait. Genies and cyborgs ...? Huh?"

He smiles amusedly as he climbs into bed

beside me and rolls over onto his side, facing me. "I kind of like that you don't know a lot about our worlds, and that I get to be the one to show you everything. I know you haven't seen much yet, but I promise, when we travel, I'll show you everything, including this band performing live."

For once in my life, I'm actually bursting with excitement about something.

"I'd like that, Fost. I really would." When the most real smile I've ever seen graces his pretty lips, I ask, "What?"

"It's nothing." He shakes his head, his grin as shiny as the stars and moon outside. "It's just that you called me Fost."

"Your family does, too," I remind him, unsure what the big deal is.

His grin continues to sparkle. "I know, but I like that you're using my nickname. It means you're getting more comfortable around me."

I neither deny or admit it, unsure about the answer myself.

"I'm so tired tonight," I mumble through a yawn.

"You should go to sleep. You had an exhausting day." He lightly grazes his lips across my forehead and my heart does that stupid fluttering thing again. "You're safe with me."

Safe.

Safe.

Safe.

He wants me safe.

"Goodnight, Fost," I whisper as exhaustion pulls me under.

"Goodnight, beautiful girl," he whispers so softly I wonder if I heard him correctly. "I'm so glad I finally got to meet you."

Again, his words puzzle me.

"What do you mean by finally ...? I think ..." I fight the sleepiness inside my body, yet it's too powerful to overcome, and I have no choice but to succumb to it.

CHAPTER 10

THE NEXT DAY PASSES BY IN A BLUR, AND IS mostly filled with practicing using my powers while we wait to hear from Emaline about the room of darkness.

After we're done practicing, Easton decides we need to have some fun, mostly because he's bored.

I'm learning that he's bored a lot and likes to let everyone know when he is.

"No thanks," Foster immediately turns down Easton's suggestion of having a little fun and doing something crazy.

He and I are sitting on a sofa in the living room and a fire is blazing in the fireplace, the flames created by Foster's power. Music is playing from a stereo, a song by the band *Ash East Arrow*. I like the sound of their music, although their pained and tortured filled lyrics make me worry how frightening some of the other worlds are.

Easton fires a playful glare at Foster as he plops down in a chair across from us. "Why the instant rejection, brother?"

Foster drapes his arm across the back of the chair. "Because, usually when you want to have fun, we end up doing something stupid like burning up an entire field or accidentally opening a portal to the Underworld."

My eyes widen. I don't even know why. I've heard so much crazy shit lately that nothing should faze me anymore. "The Underworld actually exists?"

"I love how she skipped over the fact that we accidentally opened a portal to it." Easton kicks his feet up onto a table and tucks his hands behind his head. "Come on; let's do something fun. I'm bored."

Foster ignores him, looking directly at me. "The Underworld does exist, and it's probably one of the scariest worlds there is, at least according to most of the creatures that've been there. And when we accidentally opened that portal, that scariness leaked into our house in the form of four grim reapers. It was intense to say the least."

"*Grim reapers* exist? And there're more than one? What the actual shit?"

Chuckling, Foster places a finger underneath my chin and guides my mouth closed. "There is, but unless you play let's-see-who-can-build-a-more-powerful-orb-of-power with Easton that conclusively results in a portal to the Underworld opening up in your living room, you probably won't cross paths with one." He lowers his hand to his lap. "They mostly stick to their world unless they're collecting souls."

"So, if I see one, then they're probably there to collect my soul?" I ask with a shudder.

He shakes his head. "Our kind's souls aren't collected by reapers."

"Then what happens when we die?" I ask, leaning back against the sofa, the back of my head ending up resting against his arm.

"When our kind die, our essences leave our bodies and return to a field a lot like the one you saw when you went into that portal with my family," Easton answers, slanting forward in his chair and resting his arms on his knees.

"That doesn't sound too bad, I guess," I tell him, stretching out my legs in front of me.

"It really isn't," Foster says, combing his fingers through my hair. "Some also believe that, when we die, our essence reunites with the essence of the creature we love."

The touch of his fingers in my hair is like a little massage and makes my eyelids feel heavy. "That doesn't sound too bad at all."

"You know what does sound bad, though?" Easton asks with a cock of his brow. "The sound of your guys' lust flowing down the link. Seriously, turn that shit off."

I scowl at him. "I wasn't feeling lustful." *Was I?*

"You may not have been, but this guy over here." Easton hitches his finger in Foster's direction.

Foster blasts his brother with a glare. "Not that shit off. Seriously. I can't take it anymore."

"You knock it off," Easton quips. "It's making me want to puke all over the floor."

I smirk at him. "Puke on the floor. Like we care. All that will result in is you having to clean puke off the floor."

Easton mirrors my smirk. "Like I care either. I

wouldn't even have to lift a finger to do so." His smirk morphs into an arrogant grin as he snaps his fingers.

A shimmering wave rolls over the room, wiping the dust away and making all the furniture, walls, floor, and mantle sparkle.

Feeling a little haughty myself, I lift my hand and think about the idea of a cloud appearing above him and showering rain down on him. We practiced enough that I'm fairly sure I can do it.

As a cloud forms above him, I start to grin, but then the cloud crumbles and lands on Easton, covering him in smoky dirt.

He curses, jumping to his feet and wiping the dirt off his face. "What the hell was that?"

I pull a *whoops* face. "Not what I was going for, but it still sort of got the job done."

Easton drags the back of his hand across his face, wiping away the dirt from his lips as he narrows his eyes on me. "So, you want to play dirty, do you?"

Shit. I so didn't think this through all the way. "No, not really."

An eerie smirk possesses his face as silver sparks of light hiss across his skin. "You probably should've thought about that before you dumped a cloud of dirt on me, lightning eyes." Then he raises his hands.

Fear lashes through me. Not that I think Easton will do anything to hurt me, but I'm sure whatever he's about to do isn't going to be nice either.

I jump to my feet, preparing to run.

His smile broadens as he stalks toward me. "Chasing is only going to make this more fun."

Panicking, I try to drag my powers out of me, but the panic is making the energy inside me falter. Luckily, Foster stands up and positions himself in front of me.

"Move out of my way, Fost," Easton gripes. "I just want to play with her for a while."

Foster crosses his arms. "No fucking way."

"I'm not going to hurt her," Easton says, sounding hurt.

"I know, but ..." Foster takes a breath. "I just can't let you do this, okay? It goes against all of my instincts."

"Oh, fine. Ruin my fun." Pouting, Easton trudges out of the room with his shoulders slumped. Right as he reaches the doorway, though, he sneaks a smile at me then snaps his fingers.

Water pours down from the ceiling and spills across me. I let out a squeal, stumbling into Foster.

"You little shit," I growl out at Easton, water dripping down my face and soaking my clothes.

Easton takes one look at me, particularly the blue sparks zapping from my fingertips, and high-tails it out of the room, laughing his ass off.

Sighing, Foster reels around toward me. "Are you okay?" He looks like he's on the verge of laughing.

I wring my hair out. "This isn't funny."

"It sort of is." His smile breaks through as I glare at him. "I'm sorry, but you did dump a cloud of dirt on him, which was pretty badass, by the way."

"Yeah, it was, except for I was trying to make it rain on him."

"You'll get better," he promises, tugging on a strand of my wet hair. "And if it makes you feel any better, the whole wet look looks really good on you." His gaze deliberately scrolls up and down my body.

I roll my eyes, but heat rushes through me. Not wanting him to see me blush, I raise my chin and turn for the doorway.

"I'm going to change," I announce. "And then I'm going to bed."

"You want me to sleep with you again tonight?" The chuckling in his tone makes me want to say no. But ever since he started spending the night in my bed, nightmares of darkness have been less prominent. Plus, I like having him lay next to me, of knowing I'm not alone. Whether that makes me needy or not, I don't have a clue.

"Yeah, okay," I say, then haul ass out of the room before he can see how much I want him to sleep by me.

About an hour later, I'm showered and lounging around in my bed when a knock sounds on my door.

"Come in," I call out, figuring it's Foster.

But when the door opens, Easton steps inside.

He's wearing a pair of black pajama bottoms and a grey T-shirt, and his hair is a little damp.

"Hey," he says, raking his fingers through his hair and glancing around at the photos I hung up on the wall of my past life. Or well, it's starting to feel like my past life.

When his gaze skims across one of Gage, Nina, and I having a snowball fight and laughing our asses off, a small smile tugs at his lips. "You look happy in this one."

"I was." I scoot to the edge of the bed, stand up, and make my way over to him. "It was a couple of years ago and my mom took the photo without us knowing... I think it was the first photo she ever took of me." I press my lips together, suddenly aware of how true my statement is.

How did I never notice this before? That my parents never took photos of me?

Easton's gaze glides toward me and his lips part. I wait for him to ask me questions about what I said, if my parents were shitty, but all he says is, "Your hair's still wet."

I fidget with the ends of the strands, running my fingers through them. "Not from the water you dumped on me. I took a shower to wash that off." I scowl at him, but my lips threaten to turn upward.

I'm not sure why, but it's difficult to stay pissed off at him, even after he dumped water on me. Maybe it's because he's usually smiling and joking around.

"I don't want to sound rude, but why are you in my room?" I ask.

He shrugs. "Fost sent me in here. Max just sent him a message and said he needed his help with something." He makes a path around my room, examining more of the photos on the walls. "He asked me to come in here and lay down with you while you fall asleep." He turns toward me, tapping his fingers against the sides of his legs. "I'll only stay though if you want me to."

"Wow, is that your way of trying to be a gentlemen?" I joke in an attempt to lighten his sullen mood.

The corners of his mouth twitch. "It's a rare occurrence, but it sometimes happens. Like a eclipse or the stars aligning."

My brow teases upward. "So I should consider myself lucky?"

He grins. "Absolutely."

I grin back at him. But the corners of my mouth tip downward again when he plops down onto my bed and tucks his arms behind his head, totally comfortable.

When I make no effort to join him, his lips pull up into an impish half-grin. "Don't look at me like that. I don't bite."

"I have a feeling that's a lie," I mumble, but climb onto the other side of the bed.

He pivots onto his side, propping up onto his elbow and resting his chin against his hand. "You seem nervous," he remarks.

I make a big show of rolling my eyes. "Why would I be nervous?"

"I have no idea," he says with surprising seriousness. "You know, most of the stuff I say is just me messing around, right?"

With a yawn, I pull a blanket over me then stare up at the ceiling, feeling a light buzzing sensation just underneath my skin. I find it strange but relaxing, along with the faint scent of rain lingering in the air. *Is it coming from him?* "Yeah, why?"

"I just want to make sure you don't think I'm being serious when I tease you. I rarely am serious."

I tilt my head toward him. "Why is that?"

"Why is what?" He acts like he doesn't know what I'm talking about, but I think he does.

"Why do you joke around all the time?"

"Why does anyone joke around all the time?"

"Aw, the old answering a question with a question. Usually that means someone's hiding something."

He dismisses me with a flick of his wrist. "Nah, I'm the most straightforward creature you'll ever meet. I say whatever's on my mind whenever I want," he says then changes the subject. "We should get some sleep. It's fucking exhausting keeping an eye on you, lightning eyes." Hilarity rings in his tone.

"You're equally as exhausting," I quip, rolling onto my side.

He stays quiet, pretending to go to sleep. And yes, I know for a fact he's pretending. Maybe I would've asked him why if tiredness hadn't grabbed me by the hand and yanked me into dreamland.

I DREAM OF BEING IN A LIGHTNING BOLT AGAIN, of wearing a crown on my head, only this time I'm alone.

"You're the only one who can save them," the lightning whispers to me. "Find the others and save them."

"What are you talking about?" I whisper to the lightning. "Save who? And find who?"

"You'll know what to do when the time is right." The lightning crackles around me. "You're the strongest one."

"Strongest one of what?" I ask, diving farther into the lightning.

When I get no response, I feel as though my chest is going to tear apart, as if something has been stolen from me.

"Come back, please," I whisper, tears spilling from my eyes. "Don't leave me."

The only response I get is silence.

"DON'T LEAVE ME," I SPUTTER AS MY EYELIDS spring open and I bolt upright.

Warm hands touch my shoulders. "Easy, Sky," Foster says as he sits up in the bed beside me. "Take a deep breath."

I obey, breathing in and out until my nerves have settled down.

The sun is rising just outside and faint soft orange-pink light filters in through the window, cascading across Foster's face and the concern pouring from his lightning blue eyes.

"When did you climb into my bed?" I ask. "Where's Easton?"

"We traded places after I got back from

helping Max with a job thing. I hope that's okay." He watches my reaction closely.

"It's fine," I assure him. "I just asked because I was confused."

His gaze traces the angles of my face. "What were you dreaming about just barely? Darkness?"

I brush the tangled strands of my hair out of my face. "The opposite actually. I dreamt of lightning."

A crease forms between his brows. "Really?"

I nod. "Have you ever dreamt of that before?"

He shakes his head. "I haven't, but since lightning is our main power source, I'm guessing it's not a bad thing to dream about it. But you seemed scared when you woke up."

"I was just upset that the lightning left me."

I tell him a bit more about my dream.

He taps his finger against his lips, contemplating something. "Your dreams ... the way you describe them makes them sound like they're very vivid."

"They kind of are." I think of the fear I felt when the lightning left me. And then, of course, there's the fear I feel when darkness appears in my dreams.

"I almost wonder if maybe you have an ability

that materializes through your dreams."

"What sort of ability?"

"I'm not sure, but we can talk to my parents about it when they get back. They know more about this stuff than I do."

Speaking of his parents...

"Have you heard from either of your parents yet?" I ask, kicking the blanket off me and arching my back as I stretch.

"Yeah, actually Easton texted me a bit ago and said my mom finally got ahold of the headmistress. And she assured my mom that what happens in the room of darkness stays in the room of darkness, so unfortunately, we have to go to school today."

"What happens in the room of darkness stays in the room of darkness, huh?" I pretend not be bummed out about having to go back to school, but I kind of am. "Sounds like the rules of *Fight Club*."

"What's *Fight Club*?"

"It's a movie." I pause. "Do you guys watch those?"

"We do occasionally, but honestly, we're pretty busy with practicing sessions, school, jobs, and helping take care of our world when we need to. We barely have time to do ordinary things."

"I kind of got that already. And I'm sure having

me around is making it worse."

"Having you here is one of the best things that's ever happened to me." Quickly stroking his fingers across my cheekbone, he withdraws his hand and scratches at his cheek. "I need to go shower and get ready for school." He wets his lips with his tongue, hesitating, then a grin spreads across his lips. "Want to shower with me?"

I give him an unimpressed look, but my lips fight to turn upward. "You know, you're getting as bad as Easton."

"Hey, I heard that!" Easton shouts from outside my bedroom door. "And that's a good thing! It means he's finally getting some game!"

"He's such a drama queen," Foster mutters, his cheeks a little flushed.

"You know, him and my friend Nina would probably get along really well." I climb out of bed, tugging at the hem of my shirt. "She's equally as dramatic. Then again, they might just end up killing each other."

"Probably the latter. East doesn't usually play nice with others like him. He needs to be the center of attention."

"I hate that."

"Me, too."

We share a smile, and then he heads to leave.

I almost hate to see him go. Being around him is starting to get so comfortable.

"Foster," I call out as he opens the door. He pauses, glancing back at me with his brows knit. "Thanks for sleeping with me again." As soon as the words leave my lips, I blush while Foster grins. "I mean, thanks for ... You know what? Never mind."

Chuckling, he walks back toward me and sweeps a strand of my hair out of my eyes. "Thanks for sleeping with me, too." He winks then leaves the room, laughing under his breath.

Sighing at my spazzy-ness, I close the door then grab a pair of jeans and a black top with boots to match. Then I head out of my room and into the bathroom to take a shower. Once I'm dressed and my hair is done, I wander downstairs to make my own breakfast, something I've been promising myself I'm going to start doing. But, as with every day this week, when I enter the room, Charlotte has already made breakfast.

Easton and Foster are already there too, which is a bit odd. Usually, they take longer than me to get ready.

Foster hands me a plate stacked with French

toast as I walk in. "Breakfast is on the go today." He grabs his bag from off the counter and slings the handle onto his shoulder. His hair is a bit damp, and he's rocking dark jeans and a black T-shirt. "We have to be at the school a little early because Easton has practice."

I glance at Easton, who's stuffing his mouth with French toast. "Practice for what?" I ask him curiously.

"Cheerleading." He grins, looking pretty pleased with himself. "I look amazing in a skirt."

I restrain a smile, putting on my best dead serious expression. "I can actually see that."

His brow meticulously elevates. "You think I seem like the cheerleading type and that I'd look good in a skirt?"

"Yeah, you seem really peppy, and I bet you're legs look super cute in those uniforms." I grin when he gives me a disgusted look.

"I'm going to pay you back for that one," he warns with a smirk as he hitches his bag over his shoulder. "For the record, though, my practice is for the water team."

"Is that like a fancy word for swimming?" I ask, quickly dumping more syrup onto my French toast.

"Nope. It's water shape-shifting." When my eyes grow huge, a pleased grin etches across Easton's face as he steps toward me. "You should come watch me. I'm really good at it. Plus, you'll get to see me shirtless, so that's a bonus."

More than curious to see what water shape-shifting looks like, I nod. "Okay, I will. It actually sounds really fun."

His eyes dance with amusement. "Me being shirtless?"

"Nah, that part I'm not looking forward to at all," I give a shudder.

"Lies." Grinning, he stuffs a piece of French toast into his mouth. The entire damn thing. Then he wipes off his hands and deliberately reaches for the hem of his shirt. "I can take it off for you right now. You don't have to wait." Then he starts to lift up his shirt.

My lips part with a snarky remark. But Foster interrupts me.

"We should get going or you're going to be late," he tells Easton, then lines his palm to the small of my back and urges me toward the doorway.

"Yes, Mom." Easton strolls toward the doorway, calling over his shoulder, "Don't worry, lightning eyes, you'll still get to see me shirtless sometime."

"No thanks," I say. "I don't want to risk my retinas getting burned from seeing, what I'm betting is a very pasty, hairy, skinny chest.

"Ha! My chest is far from pasty, hairy, or skinny." Right before he exits the room, he spins around and lifts up the hem of his shirt, flashing me. "See sexy." He drags his hand across his chest and abs and I hurriedly look away.

"No, it's not—"

He walks out before I can finish, looking pretty damn cocky.

"He's so annoying," I grumble, shifting the handle of my bag higher onto my shoulder.

"Yeah, he is." Foster agrees, then steers me out of the kitchen and into the foyer where he collects his car keys from off the table.

Then he puts eye drops in my eyes and his and we head outside and get into the car.

The car ride is pretty quiet, Foster seeming distracted and Easton is busy texting on his phone. But as we're cruising down the road and I'm stuffing my face with French toast, Foster's stomach suddenly lets out the loudest rumble.

I pause mid-bite, latching onto the opportunity

to break the maddening silence. "Are you hungry?" I ask him.

He shakes his head. "Nah, I'm good."

"He's so full of shit. He didn't eat breakfast," Easton tells me, sliding forward in the seat and putting his phone away.

I move the forkful of French toast I was about to eat toward Foster's mouth. "Here. Have some of mine."

"I'm good," Foster insists. "I'll just grab something from the vending machines."

I leave the fork right where it is. "Just take the bite. There's more than enough on this plate."

His gaze slides to mine, and then he reluctantly opens his mouth and I stick the French toast in it, getting a glob of syrup on his lips. He licks it up, looking at me for an unnerving amount of time before focusing back on the road.

"Thanks."

"You're welcome." I take another bite then feed him the next one, doing it over and over again as we near the school.

"You guys are disgustingly cute," Easton whines. "Seriously, you're going to turn into one of those lovey-dovey couples, aren't you?"

Couple? We're not a couple. We're just friends.

Sure, we hold hands a lot, and he sleeps in my bed. Not to mention I just fed him breakfast. None of those things I ever did with Nina or Gage ...

Shit, we kind of do act like a couple.

"We're not ..." I trail off as Foster slows the car down at the end of at least a half-mile-long line of cars backed up from the school's gated entrance.

"What's going on?" I ask, putting the plate down on the dashboard and scooting forward in the seat.

Foster shoves the car into park. "I have no idea, but we need to find out because this looks sketchy as hell."

"Yeah, I know." Easton fishes his phone out of his pocket. "Let me text Jane. She always gets here really early and might know what's up. Although, she was ignoring my other texts this morning. Hopefully, she'll respond this time. I think she might be pissed off at me."

Foster surveys the line of cars in front of us with concern. His worry makes me anxious, which causes the clouds to react as a storm blows in and sends rain down on us.

"Shit," Foster mumbles, his gaze gliding to me

as someone honks a horn. "Sky, you need to calm down. If the storm gets too bad, everyone's going to start wondering what's causing it. Just take a deep breath, okay?"

Dammit! I'd been doing so much better lately. I thought I was starting to get the hang of controlling my powers.

"I'm sorry," I tell him. "I don't know why I'm losing control of them so badly right now."

"You're fine. Just keep taking deep breaths." Foster shuts off the engine, twists to face me, and cups my face between his hands, his skin warm against mine. "Just try to focus on being calm, like when we were in the bathroom the other day and your powers were at peace."

"But we built a little world when that happened," I remind him, draping my hand over my waist.

"I'll make sure nothing builds this time," he swears, his gaze intense. "Just take a few deep breaths and focus on connecting with my powers. It'll be good practice for you, okay?"

I nod and do as he instructs. *Air in. Air out. Calm. Calm. Calm. Feel the energy around me, so connected to it ...*

He watches me as he skims his fingers along

my cheekbones, the touch having a calming effect on me. The rain shushes, the clouds parting again and letting sunlight kiss the world.

"See? No more storm. No more fear." One side of his mouth tugs upward into a gorgeous half-smile. "You're so good at this. You know that? Seriously, I bet, in just a couple of months, you'll be better than I am."

"I'm not that great," I tell him. "You're just good at telling me what to do."

"Maybe we're just good together," he suggests, tangling his fingers through my hair.

"Dude, if you two are going to make out for the first time, please don't do it in front of me," Easton breaks the moment like ... well, like only Easton can. "And do us all a favor and try to block out that sexual tension between you two. It's beyond uncomfortable knowing how much you guys want to screw each other." He throws a joking smile at us.

"Maybe you shouldn't listen to it then," I quip with a sugary sweet smirk. "I'm sure it's happened enough times at this point that you can just block them out if you want to."

Easton's lips span into a mischievous grin as he

slants closer to me. "You do realize you just admitted you want to fuck Foster, right?"

Huh....

I replay what I just said.

Dammit!

I face the window, letting my hair veil my flushing cheeks. "That's not what I meant."

"You're such an asshole sometimes, East," Foster says then glances at me. "Sky, just ignore him. You know he gets off on it."

"I know." But I'm unable to look either of them in the eyes.

Not until my cheeks stop feeling like they're going to erupt into flames.

Foster fixes his finger underneath my chin then angles my head toward him. "It's okay. You don't need to be embarrassed. It's just Easton and I in here with you and neither of us care."

"That's easy for you to say. You're not the one who embarrassed yourself a ton of times around me." I shift in the seat, scratching my wrist. "I, on the other hand, have embarrassed myself a lot around you. Like the first time we spoke, amongst many other times. And all the times I asked you to sleep with me."

He drops his hand to his lap, and his gaze

descends as he mutters, "The first time we spoke ... it didn't happen like you think it did."

I recall something he said to me the other night about liking me. "What do you mean?"

His eyes flicker with light as he looks up at me. "When you approached me that day, it wasn't the first time—"

"No, no, no, no, no," Easton blurts out as he grips the life out of his phone. "Fost, we have to go. *Now.*"

Foster rips his gaze off me. "Why?"

Panic flares in Easton's eyes. "Jane just texted me back, and apparently, a whole army of hunters showed up earlier today, through portals, took over the school, and trapped everyone already inside."

My heart thunders inside my chest, and above, the sky booms. But they are too preoccupied to notice.

Calm down, Sky. Panicking isn't going to help.

"Dammit," Foster growls out, strangling the life out of the steering wheel. "How the hell did they get access to portals?"

"I have no damn idea," Easton shakes his head. "But we're lucky we were running late today or we might've been locked in there, too."

Foster hurries and revs up the engine. "Does

the council know or are they still being silent?"

"I have no idea." Easton yanks his fingers through his hair, the strands sticking up. "This is bad, Fost. Really bad. We need to get the hell out of here and then message Mom."

Foster presses on the gas, backing up a bit. "Why didn't anyone warn us about this before we showed up here? And everyone else for that matter?"

"Because no one on the outside of the school knows what's going on yet," Easton explains, his gaze tracking the land and cars around us. "Everyone who made it inside the school has been put on lockdown and can't communicate with anyone outside. The only reason Jane could text me is because of her gift."

"What's her gift?" I work to breathe evenly, to not freak the hell out.

"Controlling energy that flows through electronic devices," Easton explains then glances worriedly at Foster. "But she said the hunters put a blocking spell up around the school and it's making everyone's powers weak. She could barely get the text out to me, and that's why she wasn't answering any of my messages earlier." He slumps in the seat, his jaw working from side to side. "Everyone's just trapped in there with them. We need to do something. We're more powerful than them. There has to be a way to overthrow them."

Foster glances at the school then back at Easton. "Send out a text to everyone you know and those on the school's directory. That way, no one else will go inside. Then message Mom and send out an emergency signal to everyone we trust. Tell them we need to gather somewhere and make a plan on how we're going to get into the school. We're going to have to be careful since, once we get inside those walls, we won't be able to use our powers." He cranes the wheel to turn the car around. "What I don't get is why the hunters are here and how they suddenly got in the school. Are they gathering subjects for the experiments or is it for another reason? And how did they even get in with all the spells around this place ...? They shouldn't have been able to, even through a portal."

Rain drips down and splatters against the dirt as my fear elevates and my control nosedives. I don't know what to say. What to do. And this overwhelming helplessness is consuming me. I want to be stronger. I want to be as powerful as Foster believes I am—as I want to be. But I'm not there yet and I'm panicking.

My heart thunders in my chest. So does the sky. But neither of them seem to notice.

"Unless something powerful tore the protection spells down," Foster says abruptly as he backs up the car as far as it'll go. "Can you ask Jane if something else is in there with them?"

"No ... the connection's lost." Easton's fingers are hovering over his phone screen. "I'll text Mom and Dad and let them know. Maybe they'll be able to give us a few ideas."

Foster shoves the shifter into drive. "You should send a text to our brothers, too, just in case the hunters plan on trying to raid more places. Tell them to meet us at the house for now. We have enough protection spells up that we should be safe there for a bit. At least until we can figure out what's going on."

Easton stops typing and glances up at Foster. "You don't think the hunters are after us, do you?" His gaze travels toward the school then to the line of vehicles, some of which are trying to turn around. "Maybe they're trying to capture us. It'd be easier to do while we are here and not around our family."

"You don't think they're after me, do you?" I interrupt. When Foster tosses a questioning look at me, I add, "A couple of nights ago, I had a dream with hunters and darkness in it, and darkness said they were coming to get me. And since you said maybe I have some sort of ability connected to my dreams ..." I shrug, unsure if I'm overthinking things or not or where I'm even going with this.

"Usually dreams of darkness are just dreams, little taunting whispers that feed off your fears, which might be why the hunters were in it. But I've been wondering why your dreams are so vivid ..." Fear unexpectedly flickers in Foster's eyes. "Fuck, what if you have a dream seer ability? It's rare, but ..." Shaking his head, he shifts the car's gears and presses down on the gas, suddenly seeming more frantic to get out of here.

"What is that?" I ask loudly over the rumble of the engine. "A dream seer ability?"

"The ability for others to visit your dreams and you can visit dreams as well," Easton explains, gripping onto the back of my seat as the car lurches forward. "No one can touch you while you're there, but they can send you messages and talk to you if they realize they're in your dreams or you're in theirs."

Well, that sounds weird and creepy. "I don't think that's ever happened to me before."

"Some of the more powerful abilities manifest later in life, and since your powers have been so restrained with that wall around you that's now cracking, things might just be surfacing. Plus, you're so damn powerful ..." Fear rises across Foster's face and pours through me. "We need to get the fuck out of here."

But the truck parked behind us, the SUV in front of us, and the steep drop off on one side of the road makes it complicated for him to get his car turned around. It doesn't help that I started a rainstorm that's muddying the land.

As the tires spin in the wet dirt, Foster lets out a string of curses. "Shit." He throws the car in reverse again and tries to back up, but the tires can't get traction. Sighing, he meets my gaze. "Sky, baby, I know this is really fucking scary, but you have to try to calm down and let the sun through to dry up the ground, okay?"

"I'm trying. But I can't get it to stop ..." I pause, question marks popping up everywhere. "Did you just call me baby?"

His eyes slightly widen. "Yeah, sorry. It accidentally slipped out. I think Porter is rubbing off on me or something."

"Does he call people baby a lot?" I flinch as

hail plinks against the glass.

He nods, peering up at the cloudy sky with a frown. "That and honey and sweetheart and every other cheesy endearment possible." His gaze shifts back to me, and then he unbuckles his seatbelt. "We need to calm you down." He reaches for me. To do what, who knows, but probably something that requires a lot of touching.

But I never do find out because Easton shouts, "No, what we need is a fucking portal!" His eyes are fastened on something on the other side of the windshield. "*Now!*"

I turn to see what has him panicking, only to regret that I ever looked.

Tendrils of shadowy smoke have curled across the land, so thick I can barely see anything. Just like the other night in my dream.

"Darkness," I whisper in horror.

Foster pales as he stares at me, terror possessing him, as if he suddenly sees me in a different light, as if he's afraid of me.

I prepare myself to be kicked out of the car. After all, the guys have stressed more than a few times that they'll do whatever it takes to protect their brothers. If darkness is after me, then they'll be safe if they ditch me.

When Foster splays his fingers across my cheek, I flinch.

"We're going to get you out of here," he promises. "Nothing is going to happen to you, but I need you to stay as calm as possible, okay?"

I nod, relief washing over me like the rain outside.

"As lovely as this little moment is, we need to go," Easton warns. "Now, Romeo."

Foster's and my attention snaps back to the window, and then we freeze in horror.

The tendrils of smoke are close; wisps of evil reaching for our car.

"Drive forward into the field while I try to work on creating a portal." Easton's palms ignite with vibrant silver flames while droplets of water dew on his skin.

Foster slams his foot down on the gas, and the tires spin before the car jerks forward, ramping off the edge of the road and bottoming out in the field. My seatbelt locks from the impact, my teeth clanking together as my jaw pops.

"Everyone, hang on!" Foster shouts out a little too late.

Still, I clutch the sides of the seat and hold on as he gives the car gas. But with the muddy ground, we're not speeding up very quickly and the darkness is gaining on us, reaching for the car.

"My queen, can you hear me?" Darkness laughs inside my mind. *"Join me now. If you don't, you'll die."*

"Shut up." I throw my hands over my ears, trying to block it out, but the laughter only grows louder.

"Block it out, Sky," Foster begs as he speeds toward the trees. "Don't let it get to you, okay?"

"I'm trying." But darkness is seeping into the cracks of my mind, spinning a web of doubt and calling to a power I never thought I had, a darkness in my veins that begs to spread a plague across the land.

"East, how's the portal coming?" Foster guides a hand away from my ear then tangles his fingers through mine, his touch sparking heat through my veins and making the darkness within me flicker.

"I'm trying to get one up, but I think—"

Easton curses over the crackling of sparks.

"Fuck! I think the darkness is messing with my powers."

Foster's gaze zips to the side of me, and fear reflects in his eyes. "Well, block it out."

"I'm trying!" Easton shouts. "But it's powerful,

like it's the goddamn god himself or something ..."
He trails off, gulping. "What if it is the god of darkness himself? Because it feels really, *really* powerful, man ... Like the end of the world."

"But, why would he be here ...?" Fear abruptly pulsates off Foster as he glances over his shoulder at Easton while continuing to floor the car across the field. "You don't think that maybe when Mom talked to the headmistress, the hunters had already taken over the school, do you? Because, if so, she may have lied about the room of darkness being secure."

A slamming heartbeat of silence goes by.

"We need to get her the hell out of here," Easton whispers, his wide eyes landing on me.

My body turns to ice, goosebumps sprouting across my flesh.

The god of darkness is here?

For me?

It knows what I am.

I'm going to die.

"You're not going to die," Foster vows to me, leaving me to wonder if I said my thoughts aloud or sent my feelings down the link. "I won't let that happen." His gaze sears into me and, down the link, I feel that he means what he says.

That he'll do whatever he can to stop me from dying.

But I hate how helpless I feel.

Maybe if I unleashed some of my powers, I could hurt darkness—

Foster's gaze darts to something behind me.

I turn my head to see what he's looking at, and my heart nearly stops.

The tendrils have found us and are brushing against the car, working to get into the cracks of the windows and vents.

I open my mouth to scream as one squeezes through the vent and billows toward me, reaching for me, wanting to drag me into the darkness where I'll use my power for only bad, for—

Foster swats it away. Then, keeping one hand on the steering wheel, he uses his other hand to cup the back of my head. When his gaze melds with mine, remorse fills his eyes. "I'm so sorry about this."

Fear whiplashes through me as I prepare to be shoved out of the car, but instead he leans toward me. Sparks are showering in his pupils as he crashes his lips against mine and I gasp. He lets out a groan as he sweeps his tongue into my mouth and deepens the kiss and heat spills through my veins, pulsating through me, and my heart rate quickens. My chest warms, glowing with heat, and sparks zap through my body as his power mixes with mine. The potency of it is so overpowering that I swear I'm going to ignite.

"Let your power out," Foster breathes against my lips. "Let it all the way out. Don't be afraid. It's like creating our own little world again, only it's going to be a portal. I know you can do it. You're powerful. We're powerful. More powerful than him. Do you understand?"

I nod, even though I'm not fully sure I believe him. But I do what he says and just let everything go. Let everything I've ever felt all out. Let it connect with the world. With the elements.

When he kisses me again, I feel his power all the way through me. I feel the power of the kiss. And, as a bright ball of blue light abruptly pierces the air and swallows up the darkness, and us right along with it, I wonder if my powers and freed emotions swallowed up the entire world.

"You may have escaped me this time, Sky, but I will find you," darkness whispers to me. *"And either you can join me or you'll join the other gods and goddesses."*

I scream before silence overtakes me.

CHAPTER 11

THE NEXT THING I KNOW, MY HEAD IS throbbing and my eyes are closed. I need to move, so I force my eyes open and blink a few times, expecting to either be dead or squeezed in the passenger seat of the wrecked Camaro. But nope. The first thing that comes into focus is a glittery blue ceiling.

That has to mean I'm alive, right? Or maybe this is part of the afterlife or wherever elemental protectors go after they die.

Confused, I tilt my head to the side and take in my surroundings. I'm lying on a four-poster bed in a bedroom with black walls and a fireplace. A blanket is pulled over me, and the curtains lining the bed sway in the light breeze whispering in through the cracked open window. The air smells heavenly, like freshly fallen rain, a crackling fire, crisp snow, and a summer breeze. Basically, just like Foster.

Lost beyond imaginable, I glance toward the other side of the room and quickly discover why the air smells so wonderful.

Foster is lying down on a velvet sofa, his head resting on a pillow. His eyes are shut, and his arm is draped over the side. He looks so peaceful and relaxed, so I'm assuming we're not dead and in the afterlife or wherever.

Seeing him like this, so at ease, ignites a power inside my chest as the memory of what his lips felt like against mine burns in my mind.

Tossing the blankets off, I climb out of bed and pad across the room until I reach the sofa. As I stare down at him, watching his chest rise and fall with his breaths, my fingers itch to touch him. And my lips.

Even though I know I shouldn't, my fingers drift toward his face.

The instant they graze his cheek, his eyelids lift open, his eyes glazed over with remnants of dreamland. Blinking a few times, he focuses on me.

I start to pull my hand back because, *hello*, I

was touching him in his sleep and being a total creeper, but he places his hand over mine and traps my hand against his cheek.

"Hey." Exhaustion seeps into his tone, yet he smiles. "You're awake."

I can't help smiling back. "So are you."

He chuckles then sits up and lowers his feet to the floor. "I didn't mean to fall asleep. I was keeping an eye on you, and I guess I was more tired than I thought."

"How long have I been out?" I wonder, sitting down beside him.

"A couple of days," he says with a frown. "We were starting to get really worried about you."

"A couple of days?" I shake my head, stunned. "I've been out for that long? What happened?" My heart slams against my chest. "Wait, is Easton okay?"

He nods, rubbing his hand across the back of his neck. "East's fine. We've been taking turns keeping an eye on you. For a minute, we were worried that you..." He shakes his head. "You're awake now, though, so everything's okay."

Is it, though? Because I'm not even sure what happened. Or where the hell we even are.

"Where are we?" I ask. "Because the last thing

I remember is darkness reaching for me and your lips..." Warmth flows to my cheeks as I remember what it felt like while Foster kissed me. Power. I could feel both of his powers all the way through me. I still can if I really tune in with my body. "But anyway," I clear my throat, hoping to god he can't feel what I'm feeling now. "The last I can remember was darkness whispering to me, and I ..." I shudder as coldness rolls over me. "Then I saw this blue light, and I think I passed out."

"You did." His gaze is relentless, as if he's trying to see inside me. "I think it was because you exerted your powers so much."

"Yeah, I know. That storm going on before I blacked out was intense," I say, folding my arms across my chest.

"I'm not talking about the storm," he says carefully. "I'm talking about the portal you—we created together. The portal that brought us here."

My jaw drops. "*We* created a portal?"

He nods, molding his hand to my cheek. "You and I did, and it was fucking amazing. No one has done that in a very long time."

"Create a portal?" I ask in shock.

He nods, his gaze intense. "We created a portal that led to the world of Elemental Enchantment."

I cock my head to the side. "We have our own world?"

He chuckles, his eyes lighting up. "We do. But like with Elemental, with the deaths of the gods and goddesses, as the elemental enchanters' population dwindled, so did the size of Elemental Enchantment. From what I understand, portals stopped connecting to it, and everyone just assumed it shrank into nonexistence, but apparently not."

I shake my head in bafflement. "But then, how did we build a portal that leads to it, especially when I can't even control my powers enough to turn off a damn storm?"

"Well, part of it was probably from that ... kiss." His gaze fleetingly drops to my lips. "I'm sorry that I did that. I just knew we needed a portal, and since darkness was messing with Easton's powers, I thought maybe, if I could combine our powers, we could create one. I just never thought it'd be a portal that'd take us here."

So, that's why he kissed me? And he's sorry about it?

"I'm not sorry I kissed you." Uncertainty fills his eyes. "I just didn't want it to be under those circumstances ... I've ... I've wanted to kiss you for a very long time."

He's wanted to kiss for a very long time? But he hasn't even known me for that long.

I absentmindedly touch my fingertips to my lips, recalling how his lips felt against mine, how his power felt flowing me, My very first kiss and it was amazing, even if the circumstances sucked.

"There's some other stuff I need to tell you," he says. "And I don't want to frighten you, but I don't think lying to you right now is a good option. It's better if you're prepared for what lies ahead, okay?" He waits for me to nod then slides his hands down my face to my shoulders, finally resting them on my waist. "After we got here, my mom sent us a message through a secured magical signal and informed us that headquarters sent out a warning to her that the elemental god of darkness was at the school, specifically looking for you, but that he's no longer there. No one knows why. And the hunters left, too, and left almost everyone unscathed. Thank the gods." He lets out a shaky exhale. "He's the one who broke down the protection spells around the school and created the portal so he and the hunters could get in. And like we suspected, he was the one who forced the headmistress to tell my mom it was safe for you to go back to school. No one's sure how he got the hunters to join him, but it's either from possession—which elemental protectors of darkness are really good at—or he promised them something in exchange for helping him. More than likely power."

"Can he do that?"

"He can, but that doesn't mean he will. He could just be using them because he needs help"— he appears torn—"getting ahold of you."

I shake my head in denial. "No, there's no way he could be after me. If he was, he could've taken me any time during my life. I was never protected until I went to live with you guys, so why wait until now?"

"That might not have been the case."

"What aren't you telling me?"

His Adam's apple bobs as he swallows. "My mom ... Well, the elf they hired anyway ... he found your parents. That's the mission she's been on for the last week."

Fear crushes my chest. Oh god, something bad is about to happen. I can feel it—the dread— flowing off of him. "Are they ...? Are they alive?"

He nods. "They're living in a small town in

Alaska."

Hurt whisks through me, making it harder to breathe. So, darkness was showing me the truth that day. My parents did leave me.

I curl my fingers inward until my fingernails stab into my palms. "Why did they take off? Do you know? And, why didn't they ... take me with them?" I dig my nails harder into my skin until I feel warm blood trickle out.

Pity floods his eyes, along with something else. The lights around us pop against the energy rippling through me. But he doesn't tear his gaze off me.

"I don't want to lie to you, but the truth ... it's going to hurt."

"Just tell me," I choke out, piercing my fingernails deeper into my flesh, until all I can feel is physical pain. "I need to know what happened."

He slips his fingers underneath the hem of my shirt, gently stroking my skin. "The people who raised you ... who you thought were your parents—Scott and Marla—they aren't your real parents."

Tears burn my eyes, and my bottom lip trembles, but I bottle down those damn emotions and lock them up, my fists clenched so tightly my hands are trembling. "Did they adopt me?"

He reaches up and sweeps strands of hair out of my eyes. "They were taking care of you for your aunt, the one you said you never met ... She's your real mother."

"So, my mom—Marla's sister—is my real mom?" I shake my head, gritting my teeth. "Why didn't they just tell me?"

His grip on my waist tightens. "Because... because she's not really Marla's sister."

"Then, who the hell is she?" I bite out, blood trickling from the wounds on my palms and dripping onto my wrists. "And, why did she leave me with those random people?"

He winces at my sharp, clipped tone and the snap of thunder from outside. "It wasn't random. You were sent to live with Scott and Marla because they're humans who know of our world, so they could keep you hidden amongst the humans without getting freaked out when you showed signs of your powers. They were also sealed to secrecy by a blood oath made by your real mom so they couldn't tell anyone what you are. They were also sealed to you and the wall around you, which means that, as long as they were near you, you were protected. Unfortunately, they ..." He smashes his lips together, worry cramming his features and flickering down the link.

I brace myself for whatever he's going to say, knowing with how worried he is that it's going to be awful. "Just tell me, please. Like you said, I need to know."

He frees a trapped breath then pulls me closer. No, not just closer, but to him until I'm straddling his lap.

"I just want to say first that you're not alone in this. Me, East—my entire family—are going to protect and be there for you." He places his palms on my cheeks again. "And we care about you. *I* care about you. Remember that, okay?"

I smash my lips together and nod. "I'll try."

He skims his finger along my side while holding my gaze. "Your parents were paid off by the hunters to leave you. We're not positive since Marla was pretty vague with her answers. But from what she told my mom, they received a large sum of money to go to Alaska and never contact you again."

Tears sting at the corners of my eyes, tears of hurt and anger. After all that time I spent looking for them, after insisting to everyone that they'd never leave me, that's exactly what they did.

"Why?" I manage to get out.

"Marla didn't flat out say it, but between the hunters contacting you after Marla and Scott took off, and then darkness showing up at the school, we think that the elemental god of darkness and the hunters bribed them to leave so they could weaken the protection spell to get to you, but it took some time for it to weaken. He probably showed up at the school to follow through with his plan to ... to destroy you because he probably found out from that darkness that your wall was cracking. That's what we think the darkness in the room meant when it talked about the condition you were in.

"Plus, my parents and the rest of my family were gone the day they put the school on lockdown so only me and East were near you. He could have done it at the house, but it's much easier to break down the spells around the school than it is the ones put around our house. Plus, that stupid darkness room is in the school, and he can feed off the energy in it if he needs to.

"And ... I'm really sorry about this part, but I think, when my brothers and I tried to take the wall down around you, we sort of sped up the process of him being able to get ahold of you." Guilt reflects from his eyes. "I'm so sorry. I feel so awful—we all do. I'm just glad we were late to school that day and didn't make the stupid mistake of driving around the line of cars and going right inside."

"You don't need to be sorry. None of this is any of you guys' fault." A few tears stream down my cheeks and I quickly swipe them away.

I can't believe this. That the elemental god of darkness wants to kill me. That Marla and Scott abandoned me. That they're not even my real parents.

"If anything, it's Marla's and Scott's fault," I mumble. "And my mom's for abandoning me."

"Your real mom didn't abandon you." He wipes a few tears from my cheeks with his fingertips. "She thought she was protecting you by leaving you with humans."

"What was she protecting me from, though? Darkness? Because, if so, why does he want me? Just to be his stupid queen like he said? Or is he trying to kill me because I'm an elemental enchanter?"

He gives a hesitant pause. "Do you remember how I mentioned an urban legend about how some believe that, when the gods and goddesses died, they put their power sources somewhere else?"

I nod in confusion. That wasn't what I was expecting him to say.

"Well, after I kissed you and you unleashed enough energy to create the portal, the rest of your wall collapsed, and we were able to read all the secrets hidden behind it."

"Oh." The question burns at the tip of my tongue, but it takes a lot of effort to say it. "What did you find?"

He circles his arms around my waist and holds me in place, as if he's afraid I'm going to bolt. "That almost eighteen years ago, right before the god of elemental enchanters was about to die, he sent his power into the nearest and most powerful force he could find, which happened to be your mother, who was working for him at the time."

"My mom worked for the god of elemental enchanters?" I ask in shock.

What the...

How...

What?

"Yes. Although, no one was aware of this. She kept her past hidden very well, probably to protect you." He smooths his hand up and down my back. "When the god of elemental enchanters put that force inside her, he created an actual life." He presses his lips together for a beat. "That life is you."

Oh, my God ... No ... This can't be true ... It just ...

I swiftly shake my head, my pulse soaring, my power crackling underneath my skin. "No. There's no way I could be the power of a god. It's just ... weird."

"Weird exists everywhere in our world. And I know this is a lot to take in, but what's hidden behind your wall is the truth. And it makes sense when you really think about it; how you were able to open a portal to Elemental Enchantment." He tucks a lock of hair behind my ear. "You were also sent to live with Marla and Scott until your powers were strong enough to start rebuilding our world. You are going to do amazing things, Sky, but until your powers reach full strength and the rest of the power sources are found, we have to keep you hidden. If not, things like darkness can find you and will either use your powers for evil"—he swallows audibly—"or kill you."

My queen. Darkness had called me it so many times, saying I either had to join him or die. It makes sense now ... sort of.

"How do you know there're others?" I whisper as my mind struggles to process everything.

How can this be real? How can everything change so quickly? How did I never know any of this?

How?

How?

How?

"We're not positive yet, but we're assuming the other gods and goddesses had done what the elemental enchanter god did," he explains. "Like with my brothers and you, their powers were merged by an enchantment so they could all sense each other and what they were thinking and feeling. Which means, more than likely, in their final moments before death, they all did the same thing to protect their powers."

"So, how do you find out for sure?" I ask, digging my fingernails into my palms again because I can't deal with this agonizing pain tearing at my chest. "And what about my real mom? Can I ...? Can I meet her?"

"My parents and others are looking into how we can figure out where the other gods and goddesses power sources are, but you might be our best bet since you're more than likely connected to all the power sources. But you might not be able to feel the connection to them until you learn how to control your powers better." He reaches down and pries my fingernails out of my palms, then smooths his thumb along the open, crescent shaped wounds. "Until then, we'll stay here, and you'll not only practice controlling your powers, but practice trying to open a secure portal that you can control what gets in and out. Until then, it's too dangerous to leave."

He lifts my palm toward his mouth and places a soft kiss against the sensitive flesh. It's a sweet gesture and I probably would've enjoyed it more if I hadn't just found out my life was one giant lie.

"As for your real mom," he continues, then places a kiss to my other palm. "No one's seen or heard from her in a very long time, and she wasn't at the place in the mountains like she told Marla and Scott. But, if she's still alive, we'll find her. She might know more about this, too, which will help."

I just nod, unable to form words as tears gather in my eyes. I attempt to blink them back, but end up bursting into tears. I move to climb off his lap, but he tugs me closer, pressing me against his chest and letting me soak his shirt with my tears while the sky outside weeps with me.

CHAPTER 12

I CRY MYSELF TO SLEEP, AND THANKFULLY don't dream of darkness or anything for that matter. After Foster speculated my dreams might carry a bit of the truth, I'm reluctant to ever dream again.

Eventually, restlessness compels me to open my eyes.

Foster is sleeping beside me with his arm resting on my hip, looking peaceful and gorgeous as ever

I watch him sleep for a while, finding solace in it and trying not to focus on the fact that I'm the power source for the elemental enchanter god, that I could be part of what fixes our world, that I could potentially save others from deaths like Foster's grandparents and Charlotte's husband. But it's all I think about—the possibility of what I could do and how frightening it is. Yet, in the back of my mind, I want to. I want to help others. Help the Everettsons like they helped me.

Eventually, I climb out of bed and make my way over to the window to see what Elemental Enchantment looks like.

When I lift my hand to pull back the curtain, I note the dried blood on my hands, a reminder of how much pain I'd been in when Foster told me about my parents. Or well, Marla and Scott. They almost feel like strangers to me now, even though they raised me. But technically, they didn't. Technically, I pretty much raised myself. And it had never bothered me too much before. In fact, I thought that's how things were supposed to be. But then I met the Everettsons and realized that parents are supposed to care about their kids. I wonder if that's how my life would've been if my real mom raised me. Then again, she left me with Scott and Marla so she might not be that great.

As pain tears at my chest again, my fingernails instinctively curl inward. Not wanting to reopen the gashes on my palms, I open the curtain and focus on the scene before me.

The sight is startling, yet I find some sort of serenity in it, as if I belong to it or it belongs to me. And I'm kind of glad. This place is beautiful, with a sky as blue as lightning, and a sun as silvery as the crystals on snowflakes. The leaves in the flourishing trees look like iridescent rain lingering on the ground as the sunlight peeks out from the clouds to greet it. The wind dances around in ribbons of swirls, and the grass around the house I'm in is as orange and vibrant as flames. Put it all together, and this world is all the elements combined, which makes sense since that's sort of what an elemental enchanter is.

"It's pretty, right?" Foster says as he moves up behind me.

I whirl around to face him with my hand pressed to my heart. "Holy shit, I didn't hear you get up."

His hair is a little ruffled, and his clothes are wrinkled, but the dark circles underneath his eyes are less prominent.

"I think you were a little distracted by the view." He looks at me. "It's beautiful, right?"

I nod and try not to squirm, but the way he's staring at me, as if I'm important, makes me extremely nervous. Between being one of the only elemental enchanters left, and being the power source of the god of elemental enchanters at that, how am I to ever know whether anyone really likes me for me or if they're simply sticking around to protect what I am? Maybe I was always destined to be alone, which is a miserable thought, but none-theless I can't get it out of my mind.

Foster's lips sink into a frown. "What's wrong?"

Sighing, I brush past him and plop down on the edge of the bed, tucking my hands underneath my legs. "I'm just thinking about what I am and how it's kind of a curse."

He sits down beside me, so close our knees touch and his power surges through me. "It has to be hard to deal with. But, like I said, we're going to protect you. My family and I, we won't let anything happened to you."

"I know, but between what I am and with my ... with Marla and Scott just bailing on me ... how am I ever supposed to know if anyone likes me for me?" I roll my eyes at myself. "Okay, please just forget I said that. I sound like an idiot."

"You don't sound like an idiot. You're actually handling this very maturely." He intertwines his fingers through mine and gives my hand a squeeze.

"Easton and I were honestly worried you might try to run again after I told you, but you didn't, because you're strong. You're seriously the strongest creature I've ever met." He looks down at our hands and swallows hard. "I think... I need to tell you something else."

I struggle not to cringe, but I'm concerned about how much more new information my mind and emotions can handle. "Okay."

He lifts his gaze to mine. "It might be easier if I just showed you by using my ability again. That is, if you're okay with that?"

"You want to project your thoughts into me again?" I ask, making sure I'm understanding him correctly.

He gives a wavering nod. "But only if it's okay with you."

"It's perfectly okay." It's not like it was bad the first time he did it. Just startling.

Of course, when he practically bubbles with nerves as he reaches out and places his hands on the sides of my head, I just about retract my statement. But before I can part my lips, his memories soar into me, clips and images filling my mind. Memories of him standing outside the auto body shop, of the first time he saw me, which was the same day I first saw him. How beautiful he thought I looked. How he wished he could talk to me yet knew he couldn't. How he went back to my town all the time just to get a glimpse of me. How he saw me around town, sometimes with my friends, sometimes alone, and how sad I looked—I never realized I looked that sad. How scared he was the day I approached him. How he wanted to kiss me so badly when I did. How much it hurt when he had to turn me down. How much it hurt every time he was mean to me. How excited he was when he found out what I was, but that he was also afraid. Afraid that I hated him. Afraid that he'd still be alone.

Afraid. Afraid. Afraid.

But that fear shifted into something else when he spoke to me in the bushes and continued to shift every other moment we spent together. And when he kissed me, he was still afraid, but for a different reason.

Afraid that he'd lose me.

By the time he lowers his hands, I'm breathing profusely. He looks at me, seeming a bit shy and unsure, like how I imagined he would be before I met him that day at the auto body shop.

I want to say so much to him, tell him everything, tell him anything, take away his pain, but my lips are stunned into silence. So, I do the only thing I can do.

I lean forward and press my lips against his.

He doesn't hesitate, kissing me back, his tongue slipping into my mouth. His power surges through me and my heart speeds up, fluttering like a damn lunatic. Sparks of electricity dance across my flesh and spin a web toward him, mixing with his power and sending lightning crackling through our bodies. The sensation feels good.

Really, *really* good.

No good doesn't describe this. This kiss is everything my first kiss should've been. And my second kiss. In fact, I'll probably compare every other kiss I have from now on to how wonderful his lips feel on mine.

I kiss him until I can't think straight and only pull back when I need to breathe.

"Just so you know," I whisper breathlessly. "I watched you a lot, too. In fact, I looked for your car at the shop every Friday."

He rubs his lips together, his eyes flashing with lightning. Then he kisses me deeply, his hands roving all over my body. "I'm sorry things were so shitty between us at first, but I want to make up for it," he whispers between kisses.

Then he bites on my lip, sucking on it, before pulling away to meet my gaze.

The way he's looking at me makes me feel safe and breathless. It's the most wonderful sensation I've ever felt.

"Maybe we can start over?" he asks with hope in his eyes.

I bite on my bottom lip, biting back the urge to kiss him. Not because I'm afraid to but because there's something I need to say. "I don't want to completely start over. I like a lot of the stuff that's happened between us."

He lets out a relieved exhale then leans in and welds his lips to mine.

We kiss for hours, lying on the bed with his body over mine. Our hands wander, buttons getting undone, flesh against flesh, lips against lips, our powers mixing.

By the time we come up for air the elements have taken over the room, but in a peaceful way, like the time we were in his bathroom.

He rests his forehead against mine as he works to catch his breath. My hands are resting against his bare chest. My shirt is still on, but the buttons are undone and my heart is racing, but from excitement.

"So, what do we do now?" I ask as I work to slow down my racing pulse. "I mean, what's next other than me practicing controlling my powers and opening the portal?"

"Well, with Easton stuck in here with us, we'll probably want to make that a top priority," he teases with a grin. But then he grows serious, brushing his lips against mine then dragging his teeth along my bottom lip. "I wouldn't mind, though, if we spent some time doing this."

"That sounds perfect to me." I loop my arms around him, pulling him closer, and seal my lips to his, letting myself have a small, nice moment for once, because it makes dealing with the danger I face in the future a hell of a lot easier.

Knowing I'm not alone in all of this does.

ABOUT THE AUTHOR

Jessica Sorensen is a *New York Times* and *USA Today* bestselling author who lives in the snowy mountains of Wyoming. When she's not writing, she spends her time reading and hanging out with her family.

ALSO BY JESSICA SORENSEN

Enchanted Chaos Series:

Enchanted Chaos

Shimmering Chaos

Iridescent Chaos (coming soon)

Chasing Hadley Series:

Chasing Hadley

Falling for Hadley

Holding onto Hadley

Holding onto Hadley: The Deal

Untitled (coming soon)

The Breathing Undead Series

Breathing Lies

Shadowed Whisperers (coming 2019)

My Cursed Superhero Life:

Grim

Untitled (coming soon)

Capturing Magic:

Chasing Wishes

Chasing Magic

Untitled (coming soon)

Cursed Hadley:

Cursed Hadley

Enchanting Hadley (coming soon)

Tangled Realms:

Forever Violet

Untitled (coming soon)

Curse of the Vampire Queen:

Tempting Raven

Enchanting Raven

Alluring Raven

Untitled (coming soon)

Unraveling You Series:

Unraveling You

Raveling You

Awakening You

Inspiring You

Fated by Darkness

Untitled (coming soon)

Unexpected Series:

The Unexpected Way of Falling

The Unpredictable Way of Falling

Untitled (coming soon)

Shadow Cove Series:

What Lies in the Darkness

What Lies in the Dark

Untitled (coming soon)

Mystic Willow Bay Series:

The Secret Life of a Witch

Broken Magic

Untitled (coming soon)

Standalones:

The Forgotten Girl

The Illusion of Annabella

Confessions of a Kleptomaniac

Rules of a Rebel and a Shy Girl

The Heartbreaker Society:

The Opposite of Ordinary

Untitled (coming soon)

Broken City Series:

Nameless

Forsaken

Oblivion

Forbidden (coming soon)

Guardian Academy Series:

Entranced

Entangled

Enchanted

Entice (coming soon)

Sunnyvale Series:

The Year I Became Isabella Anders

The Year of Falling in Love

The Year of Second Chances

The Coincidence Series:

The Coincidence of Callie and Kayden

The Redemption of Callie and Kayden

The Destiny of Violet and Luke

The Probability of Violet and Luke

The Certainty of Violet and Luke

The Resolution of Callie and Kayden

Seth & Greyson

The Secret Series:

The Prelude of Ella and Micha

The Secret of Ella and Micha

The Forever of Ella and Micha

The Temptation of Lila and Ethan

The Ever After of Ella and Micha

Lila and Ethan: Forever and Always

Ella and Micha: Infinitely and Always

The Shattered Promises Series:

Shattered Promises

Fractured Souls

Unbroken

Broken Visions

Scattered Ashes

Breaking Nova Series:

Breaking Nova

Saving Quinton

Delilah: The Making of Red

Nova and Quinton: No Regrets

Tristan: Finding Hope

Wreck Me

Ruin Me

The Fallen Star Series:

The Fallen Star

The Underworld

The Vision

The Promise

The Lost Soul

The Evanescence

The Darkness Falls Series:

Darkness Falls

Darkness Breaks

Darkness Fades

The Death Collectors Series (NA and YA):

Ember X and Ember

Cinder X and Cinder

Spark X and Spark

Unbeautiful Series:

Unbeautiful

Untamed

CPSIA information can be obtained
at www.ICGtesting.com
Printed in the USA
LVHW011545170520
655738LV00006B/287